Unlike th... ... ...e
torches, th... ...nding, pure glare.

It was the light of righteousness.

Her dress caught fire first. Then her skin started to blacken. The rope also ignited, and soon the corpse fell to the ground.

A huge cheer went up from the crowd. John led it.

And then for some reason the cheers started to die, even as the corpse of Matilda Dixon was now a tiny inferno. John didn't understand why, until a small voice said, "Papa?"

John Ames whirled around at the familiar voice. It was his son William. Next to him was Emma Jackson.

"We—we thought—we thought we could— could make it back before supper. We didn't—we didn't think—think we'd be so—so—so—"

And then William said nothing at all. He just stared at the burning corpse of Matilda Dixon.

A woman who had done nothing wrong.

John Ames felt a bit of himself die.

DARKNESS
FALLS

A novel by
Keith R.A. DeCandido

Based on the Motion Picture
Story by Joe Harris
Screenplay by John Fasano and James Vanderbilt

POCKET BOOKS
New York London Toronto Sydney Singapore

An *Original* Publication of POCKET BOOKS

 POCKET BOOKS, a division of Simon & Schuster, Inc.
1230 Avenue of the Americas, New York, NY 10020

ISBN: 0-7434-6632-2

First Pocket Books printing December 2002

10 9 8 7 6 5 4 3 2 1

POCKET and colophon are registered trademarks of Simon & Schuster, Inc.

For information regarding special discounts for bulk purchases, please contact Simon & Schuster Special Sales at 1-800-456-6798 or business@simonandschuster.com

Printed in the U.S.A.

Acknowledgments

Special thanks to John Hegeman and Duncan Macdonald at Revolution Studios for answering all my dumb questions; Joe Harris and Charles Adlard for *Darkness Falls: The Tragic Life of Matilda Dixon* comic book, from which I ruthlessly cribbed; the Pocket Books gang, including editor John J. Ordover and publishers Scott Shannon and Liate Stehlik; my wonderful agent, Lucienne Diver; the Web sites Victoriana.com and the Virtual Victorian House Tour at www.geocities.com/victorianlace11/ for useful reference; GraceAnne Andreassi DeCandido for her usual magnificent editorial advice; and the *Oxford English Dictionary* for reassuring me that the term *baby teeth* was already in use by the 1830s.

But most of all, thanks to Terri Osborne, who kept kicking me in the rear when I needed it most.

DARKNESS FALLS

one

1836

Matilda Dixon was baking a lemon cake when she was told that her husband was dead.

Until then, it had been the happiest day of her life. Every day was the happiest day of Matilda Dixon's life. It saved time and energy for more important things if she thought of it that way.

At first, she had thought the day she first met Captain Sonny Dixon to be the happiest day of her life.

That was later superseded by the day Sonny got down on his knee in the kitchen of Matilda's father's house and asked her to marry him.

That was, in turn, superseded by their wedding day, a glorious spring day in the field behind her father's house.

Then every day of their honeymoon became the happiest day.

Then the day they moved to Darkness Falls together, with dreams of Sonny becoming a successful whaler dancing in their heads, buying the lovely small house on the edge of the woods near the lighthouse.

Then every day of their lives together.

Sonny had taken his boat out several weeks ago on a whaling expedition. Matilda had expected him to return within the week—probably with another scrimshaw carving to add to the huge collection they had already amassed. Matilda had once joked, "When you grow tired of the sea, you can retire and be an artist."

"But my darling," Sonny had said with that wide smile that had so enchanted her, "I will never grow tired of the sea."

And then he would wrap his arms around her and pull her into an embrace. Mrs. Dixon stood a head shorter than Mr. Dixon, and so whenever they embraced, her head fit perfectly right under his chin, with his arms over her shoulders and her arms around his waist.

Of course, the real reason she wanted him to retire was so that they could have children. He kept promising her, "Just a few more trips at sea," before they would settle down to the business of a family. It was a sufficiently vague promise that did not actually bind Sonny to a particular time frame.

Matilda was, however, willing to wait. Sonny was worth it. Besides, he always kept his promises to her, even if he wasn't always quick about it. When they had first met, he had promised to make a scrimshaw with her face on it. Years went by, and she never saw it, but then, on their second wedding anniversary, he had presented it to her. "I may not be fast," he had said to her with that smile of his, "but I do get there in the end."

Most of Sonny's scrimshaws were displayed in various parts of their small house—on the mantel, on the end tables, on the kitchen shelves. But the one of Matilda, based on a portrait done of her for her sixteenth birthday, had a place of pride on Matilda's nightstand. It was the first thing she saw when she woke up in the morning and the last thing she saw before going to sleep. During the long, lonely days when Sonny was at sea, it served as a reminder of him that she treasured.

The lemon cake she was making was intended for young Samantha Wellington, who was turning eight today. Samantha loved lemons, and Matilda knew that the young girl would be happy as a clam when Matilda took it by their house.

Assuming, of course, that the rain ever stopped.

The storm had gone on for several hours. Matilda had been glad that Sonny wasn't due back for a few more days. Even so, as the storm brewed, she put the lantern in the window. Normally, she waited until sundown, but there was no sun today, and she wanted to make sure that Sonny could find his way home on the off chance that he came home early.

Not that Sonny Dixon had ever been early for anything a day in his life. But Matilda always held out hope. Without hope, she would never have survived the long weeks without her husband.

The cake was in the oven, and Matilda was struggling to figure out how to transport it in the rain to the Wellington house without ruining it, when the knock came at the door.

It couldn't have been Sonny. It was, after all, his house.

"Coming!" she called out, and headed for the door. When she left the kitchen, a chill came over her. She assumed it to be just the cold, rainy weather seeping in through the walls of the old house, only noticed as she moved away from the warming glow of the oven.

Matilda opened the door only a crack, so as not to let any more of the cold and rain in.

She saw two smartly dressed men, wearing top-coats and hats to protect them from the elements. Matilda recognized them as two men from the town, Mr. Turley and Mr. Jefferson. Both good men; Matilda remembered that Sonny had spoken highly of Mr. Jefferson in particular.

"Mrs. Dixon," Mr. Jefferson said, removing his hat, despite the weather.

"Sorry, ma'am," Mr. Turley added. He declined to remove his headgear. Matilda couldn't bring herself to blame him. The rain had grown worse in the hours Matilda had spent in the kitchen working on the cake.

"Mrs. Dixon—Matilda," Mr. Jefferson started, then stopped. He took a breath, put his top hat to his heart, looked down, and closed his eyes.

A fist of ice clenched Matilda Dixon's heart. There was simply no manner in which she could conceive that what Mr. Jefferson was about to convey was in any sense good news.

"I'm sorry to be the one to tell you this. Mr. Dixon's boat—Sonny's boat—they came up against something fierce out there. They don't think anyone survived." He finally looked up at her with pale blue eyes. "I'm sorry."

A female voice said, "That's quite all right, Mr. Jefferson, Mr. Turley. Thank you both for coming by to tell me this." Dimly, Matilda realized that it was her own voice doing the talking, though she had no conscious recollection of forming those words.

Sonny was dead.

She couldn't believe it.

She *wouldn't* believe it.

Mr. Turley finally spoke. "We're terribly sorry, Mrs. Dixon."

"Of course you are. You're good men, both of you," the female voice said. "Thank you."

"It's—it's possible he may have survived," Mr. Jefferson said, "but we didn't think it would be fair to you to—well—"

"I understand, Mr. Jefferson. Thank you."

She closed the door on the two men.

In the back of her head, the same part that acknowledged that it was she herself who spoke to the two men, Matilda recognized that she should have invited the two men in. The Dixon house was right on the coast, near the lighthouse, and a far walk from the center of town. Both men would be cold and in dire need of shelter and perhaps a cup of tea.

But Matilda couldn't bear the idea of anyone in the house. Not now. Not knowing that Sonny would never set foot in it again.

"Just a few more trips at sea." That was what Sonny

had said every time she had brought up the idea of having children, of having a family. Matilda had lived for the day when she could bake sweets for her own brood, had longed to hear the sounds of small feet pattering about their small home by the lighthouse, had desired so strongly to hear Sonny's voice telling them stories of his adventures on the sea.

Instead, he had one adventure too many.

She turned out the lantern in the living room window. Sonny would never need it to guide him home ever again.

"I may not be fast," he had said once, *"but I do get there in the end."*

Not this time, he didn't.

Or perhaps he did.

It all depended on how one looked at it, didn't it?

She went upstairs, the Wellington girl's lemon cake forgotten in the oven. She didn't look into the spare room that someday was going to be the nursery for their children. Instead, she went into the bedroom that she and Sonny had shared all too rarely. She walked over to the nightstand and picked up the scrimshaw with her face etched into the ivory.

The remnant of one of Sonny's more successful whaling expeditions, the ivory felt heavier in her hand than it ever had before.

How long she stared at the image of herself, she could not say. She had been prettier then, when she was sixteen. Sonny, of course, insisted that she grew more beautiful with each passing year.

But he was her husband. He was supposed to say things like that.

Besides, he also said that he would always come home to her.

She opened the slim drawer of the nightstand. Inside it lay several carefully folded handkerchiefs. After taking one of them out—it was mono-grammed with a lovely calligraphed "MD"—she placed the scrimshaw in the drawer amidst the remaining kerchiefs and closed it.

To her surprise, there were no tears for her to wipe away with the handkerchief, as she would have thought. Still, she kept the kerchief handy in case any came.

She went back downstairs and sat in the living room, not bothering to light any lanterns, listening to the rain fall, staring at the scrimshaws all around the house, and not feeling the cold that hovered in the air as the storm intensified.

The lemon cake was ruined.

two

1990

The blood trickled from Kyle Walsh's mouth.

He smiled.

The ten-year-old stood in the boys' bathroom of Darkness Falls School staring at himself in the mirror. Class would start any minute, but one of Kyle's teeth had come loose the previous day. The pain didn't bother him all that much, as long as he didn't bite down on it—he chewed his breakfast that morning on the other side of his mouth—but he found the occasional trickle of blood mesmerizing. It looked so odd reflected in the filthy mirror and under the slightly green-tinged fluorescent lights.

Kyle had been slow to lose his baby teeth, and this one was apparently the last to go. He had never understood why the body worked the way it did, why kids' teeth would grow in, then fall out and be replaced by new ones. Why couldn't the mouth get the teeth right the first time? Everything else was the same—bones, muscles, skin, hair. They all adjusted to the way the body grew.

But not the teeth. No, they were stubborn. They grew one way only, and then, when the rest of the body shot past them, getting bigger, getting stronger, the teeth just sat there and wouldn't budge, finally falling out of the mouth in protest.

Yes, teeth were stubborn. Kyle appreciated that. He was stubborn, too.

Of course, it was especially funny that his last baby tooth was falling out this week. After all, this was when Miss Pisapia had them doing their oral reports on the history of Darkness Falls. So far, the topics had all been the same.

Darkness Falls was, ultimately, just some boring small town like every other small town that sat on the East Coast. Lots of quaint little houses that were top-of-the-line when they were built in colonial times. Cute little shops—or, if the owners wanted to draw in more tourists, "shoppes"—that sold lots of stupid junk. Badly paved roads that were probably fine in the horse-and-buggy days but mostly just made for bumpy rides in the backseat of the car.

Kyle didn't mind that so much, but his mother was always complaining about what it did to their suspension. (His father used to complain, too, of course, until he died. Then he stopped.)

And boats.

Living in Darkness Falls, Kyle had really learned to hate boats. Not to mention that stupid lighthouse. What was it *for?* Sure, ships needed them a hundred years ago, but what did *that* have to do with anything now?

With all that, Darkness Falls wasn't much different from any old-fashioned town on the Atlantic Ocean from Nantucket to Key West.

Except for one thing.

The first bell rang, indicating that the kids had three minutes to get to their classes. Kyle wiped the blood from his chin, spit out the other blood that had collected in his mouth, then wiped his mouth again, as the residue had gotten on his lips.

Part of him was tempted to leave it there, just to see how Miss Pisapia, or one of the stupid girls like Kimberly or Anya, would react.

But that would just get him sent to the principal's office. Again. Or worse, to the guidance counselor. Kyle would have much rather sat through another stupid report about their stupid town than go see either of those two ever again.

The part that truly reeked was that he'd have to do both again. He just knew it. Not a month went by without at least one trip to both those creeps, and often more than one.

Three minutes later, Kyle was sitting in Miss Pisapia's class as she called Kimberly Schwartz to the front of the room, and he was starting to think that Principal O'Malley's office wouldn't be all that bad. (The guidance counselor, of course, would be. Since his father died, he'd spent more time with the stupid guidance counselor than with his mother.)

Kimberly had, of course, made a diorama. Teachers loved dioramas, and Kimberly loved making teachers happy, so she had devoted her life to excelling at diorama-making skills. A small Styrofoam version of the lighthouse that Kyle so hated was at the center, with blue cellophane representing the water and toy fishing boats sitting next to the toothpick-and-popsicle-stick port. And next to the lighthouse, a cardboard house, with a tiny clay figure standing in front of it. Kyle bet she was up all night working on it. Or maybe her mom and dad helped her. They were always helping her. Kyle never thought that was fair. *He* had to do his *own* homework.

Kimberly hadn't put as much energy into her speaking skills. After putting her diorama on the table at the head of the class, she stood up and started talking: " 'Why Our Town Is Famous' by Kimberly Schwartz."

She paused.

"Darkness Falls is a great place to live and not only that but it is famous, why is our town famous?, some people might ask, it is famous because of the Tooth Fairy, the—"

Miss Pisapia interrupted. "Slow down, Kimberly."

Kimberly swallowed. Kyle tried not to laugh out loud. He was also disappointed. He wanted to see how long Kimberly could go on one breath before she turned blue and collapsed onto the floor. That would've made the day worthwhile.

"The Tooth Fairy is a woman who lived here hundreds of years ago and had no husband or children and who never left town. She lived all alone up by Lighthouse Point, and she never left town."

Kyle struggled to keep a straight face at Kimberly's look of annoyance at herself for repeating that. To cover, he looked over at Cat Greene in the next row.

Cat was Kyle's best friend. That was mostly because she was Kyle's only friend. She wasn't stupid or prissy like the other girls, and she wasn't stupid and obnoxious like the boys. She actually had a sense of humor.

Which was unfortunate, because as soon as Kyle looked over at her, Cat stuck her index finger in her mouth, simulating puking.

He couldn't help but grin at that one.

Then he shut the grin down. It wouldn't do for Miss Pisapia to see that. She didn't like it when the kids smiled. It made her think they weren't paying attention—which was stupid, to Kyle's mind. If they were smiling, it meant not only were they paying attention, but they knew just how dumb everything they were learning was.

Kimberly went on. "When one of the town's children lost a tooth, the woman would go to their house at night and give them a shiny gold coin for it and she only did it for the kids in town because she never left town."

Even Miss Pisapia rolled her eyes at this third repetition of the obvious. Kyle was worried that he'd lose all his own teeth when his mouth exploded with the laugh he was trying desperately to keep in.

Kimberly, meanwhile, moved over to the diorama. She reached behind it and pulled on a couple of strings that Kyle hadn't noticed. That action prompted the toy boats to move in and out of the little Fudgsicle-derived port. Kyle bit back a comment that they didn't need to bother going to see

Back to the Future III with such great special effects right here in their very classroom.

"Darkness Falls was a fishing town and when fishermen would sail back to their homes they would tell the story of this generous old lady and the people in those other towns she never went to heard about what she was doing."

Kyle wondered why she was showing people coming *to* Darkness Falls when she was talking about people going to other places *from* Darkness Falls.

"And soon they started leaving money under their children's pillows and saying it was from 'the Tooth Fairy,' and that is why our town is famous. The End, Copyright 1990, All Rights Reserved."

A couple of the other kids snickered at that, which let Kyle chuckle without guilt, finally. Miss Pisapia didn't react to the guffaws, because she was too busy giving Kimberly one of those Teacher Looks.

"That's what they put on movies at the end!" Kimberly whined.

"Take a seat, Kimberly," Miss Pisapia said, though Kyle imagined she wanted to say something else.

He certainly did. Kimberly's report was clear and concise, had nice visual aids, and was also completely wrong.

Kyle didn't know whether to be depressed or amused.

The one thing this lousy town was good for, and people couldn't even get it right. All week, none of them had.

Miss Pisapia folded her hands on the desk. "We should all thank Kimberly for that illuminating report on a subject also covered this week by Ron, John, Anya, Larry, Amber, Emily, and Vikram."

Once again, Kyle had to keep himself from laughing. This time was even harder, because all seven of those kids looked so *thrilled* that they'd made the teacher happy. Kyle, who had spent most of his life keeping his teachers as unhappy as possible, knew full well that Miss Pisapia was sick and tired of all the stupid Tooth Fairy reports.

And so was Kyle.

"Does anyone have a history report that *doesn't* have anything to do with our town's Tooth Fairy legend?"

"I did the Civil War," Cat said.

"Thank God," Miss Pisapia muttered.

Kyle couldn't help himself. He had to say it, or he'd go even more nuts than he already was.

"They're telling it wrong, anyway."

As nasty as the Teacher Look that Miss Pisapia gave Kimberly, the one she gave Kyle now was a whole lot nastier. "And I'm sure you're now going to enlighten all of us as to the correct story?"

Shrugging, Kyle got up. "Sure."

Cat shook her head and gave him a pleading look, but Kyle ignored it. A couple of the other kids whispered and made noises—especially that jerk, Ray. Kyle ignored them, too. They all thought he was crazy anyhow, so what difference did it make if he acted crazy?

He walked over to Kimberly's stupid diorama. Reaching in, he grabbed the little clay figure, which was supposed to be the oh-so-famous Tooth Fairy.

"Yeah, the Tooth Fairy lived here. But Kim didn't finish the *real* story."

As he spoke, he yanked a piece of string off the fishing boat. It wouldn't be able to move back and forth now, and Kimberly let out a little whimper at his damaging her hard work.

"See, one night two kids went out. One of them had lost a tooth, and they went to visit the Tooth Fairy. They never came home."

Kyle started tying a slipknot with the string. He was going to show these idiots what the truth behind the legend *really* was.

"So all the men in town made up a mob. And they went up to Lighthouse Point with torches, sticks, and axes, and they dragged the old woman out of her house."

"Kyle," Miss Pisapia said, but Kyle ignored her, too, as he slipped the loop he had made with the slipknot around the tiny neck of the figure.

"They dragged her out to the lighthouse, and then they hanged her over a ship's yardarm so finally everyone could see her."

He grabbed the string about halfway up with one hand and then let go of the clay figure with the other.

"They hanged her until she was dead," he said, even as Kimberly's small figure dangled by the neck from the string. It swung back and forth like a psychiatrist in some old movie hypnotizing someone with a pocket watch.

"But that's not even the end of the story. Eventually, the missing kids turned up safe and sound. The townspeople realized they had killed this woman for *doing nothing wrong*. And this town's been screwed up ever since."

The silence that greeted Kyle's report was broken only by more whimpering from Kimberly. Actually, she was crying. Kyle desperately wanted to laugh in her face, but she was all the way in the back of the room, and he didn't want to walk that far.

From the front of the room, dopey Ray decided to open his mouth, which was always a sign of bad things.

"You're such a weirdo."

Coming from this idiot, that was a compliment. "I'm not a weirdo," Kyle said. "You're a weirdo—"

"Okay, boys, that's enough," Miss Pisapia said before Kyle could explain, in great depth, precisely why Ray was the weirdo and not he.

Ray looked at one of the other morons he hung out with. "Ever since he moved here, he's been such a weirdo dick—"

"Language, Raymond!" Miss Pisapia said sharply.

Kyle laughed. "Yeah, *Raymond."*

Ray then did something that surprised Kyle: he spit at him. It landed right on his face.

Right where the blood had been in the bathroom.

Miss Pisapia hauled herself up from her desk and put a hand on Ray's shoulder. "*That's* it. You, young man, are going to the principal's office."

The teacher droned on about how they wouldn't tolerate such behavior in the classroom.

Kyle tuned it out. He found his eyes drawn to the pile of school supplies on his desk.

In particular to the protractor for math class.

With its very sharp point.

Kyle remembered the blood he had seen under the green fluorescent lights in the boys' bathroom.

Suddenly, and for no reason that he could actually speak in words, Kyle found himself very interested in whether or not Ray's blood was as red as his own.

Miss Pisapia droned on, telling Ray what a disgrace his behavior was, Ray trying to defend himself on the basis of Kyle's character deficiencies, Miss Pisapia not buying the argument that it's okay to torment someone if you find him socially unacceptable.

Kyle walked to his desk, grabbed the protractor, and raised it into the air.

Cat Greene's eyes grew as wide as saucers. Kyle wasn't sure if she actually cried out, "Kyle, don't!" or if he just imagined that she did. He didn't really care, either. He just *had* to know what color Ray's blood was.

He brought the point of the protractor down into Ray's back.

Some noise was made in the classroom. Somebody screamed. Somebody else yelled. Cat was saying something.

Kyle didn't pay any attention to any of it. He was busy staring at Ray's back to see if his blood was red.

When he saw that it was, he smiled.

three

Days like this, Scott O'Malley felt as if he was back in Boston.

He'd grown up in the Boston public school system and had had noble intentions of giving some of what they'd provided for him back, of being the guiding force to a new generation of South End youngsters, just as his teachers were for him. They had taken a callow, shallow youth and molded him away from the Southie standard of the punk Irish kid and into a somewhat respectable adult who chose college over construction work or some other blue-collar job.

What he never realized was what a pain in the ass it would be dealing with kids like him from the other side of the desk.

He had always thought highly of his teachers

when he was a kid, but as an adult he was close to worshipping them for not actually hauling off and murdering the demons in their charge.

After several years of increased stress, he had moved up to administration, thinking—erroneously, and against the very loud objections of his wife, his kids, his father, his mother-in-law, and his psychiatrist—that it would reduce said stress and still allow him to repay the debt he felt he owed to his own teachers.

One diagnosis of high blood pressure and two ulcers later, he had finally given up and started looking for work outside the city. Way, way outside the city.

Luckily, medical history notwithstanding, he had found a position available as the principal of the primary school in the small town of Darkness Falls. A Southie born and bred, O'Malley had always thought of small towns like Darkness Falls as indistinguishable from hick farming towns in Kansas. He was surprised, then, to come for the interview and find, if not what anyone would call a thriving metropolis, a perfectly fine modern city that had such amenities as fax machines and the occasional personal computer. In fact, Darkness Falls School had a better mainframe than the public school in Boston that he'd left behind.

Best of all, the kids were *nice*. Okay, they weren't about to win Best Behaved Kids of the Universe awards or anything, but they generally weren't armed with switchblades or violent or in need of serious therapy at best and jail time at worst.

The teachers weren't exactly the best and the brightest. The curricula were no doubt cutting edge when they were first printed in 1927 but left something to be desired a mere ten years away from the twenty-first century. O'Malley had been struggling to change that, which had been difficult, but, unlike the challenges of the South End, this was more a case of getting the old guard to change its habits and was a gentle fight against tradition, not a physical fight against fists or an ideological fight against bigotry.

All in all, he was content with his life in Darkness Falls, as it was nothing like the nightmare that was being an educator in Boston.

At least until the Walsh family moved to town.

Kyle Walsh in some ways reminded O'Malley of himself as a youngster. Quiet, withdrawn, incredibly bright, and prone to nasty bouts of temper. But young Scott O'Malley had actually had friends when he was ten. Kyle's only friend was Caitlin Greene.

And now—now, he'd stabbed a boy. With a protractor, not a switchblade, but it was still giving

23

O'Malley unpleasant flashbacks to the bad old Southie days.

Dorothy Pisapia had come in blubbering like a madwoman, saying that one boy had stabbed another, and O'Malley had recovered quickly enough to calm her down, have his secretary call 911 and then the respective boys' parents, and get the nurse over to Dorothy's classroom to administer first aid until the paramedics arrived.

The ambulance arrived fairly soon and took Raymond Winchester, the victim, away to the hospital. Kyle Walsh, the perpetrator, had been sitting outside O'Malley's office since the incident, never saying a word. O'Malley noticed that there seemed to be a glob of spittle on Kyle's chin. This, he soon found out from a still-blubbering Dorothy, was what precipitated the whole thing: Ray spitting on Kyle. Dorothy didn't seem to think it was a stabbing offense, and O'Malley had to restrain himself from pointing out that he'd seen worse in his time.

But not here. Not in Darkness Falls. And even if he had, there were still going to be serious consequences.

Ray's parents arrived first. The mother had immediately gone off to the hospital to check on their son. The first thing the father—a calm, reasonable man who also happened to be one of the town's more prominent attorneys—had said was, "I assume the boy responsible for this has been expelled?"

In fact, O'Malley hadn't given it a thought yet, but he knew what the unspoken next sentence was: *If not, the lawsuit will be filed first thing in the morning.*

O'Malley spent the next fifteen minutes soothing Jeremy Winchester. Yes, the school would cover all hospital bills. No, they've had this sort of trouble from young Mr. Walsh before, sad to say—he hasn't been right since he arrived, really. Of course, the lad would be immediately expelled. That was school policy—even though, in truth, no such policy existed, simply because the idea of one student stabbing another hadn't entered into the thoughts of whoever came up with Darkness Falls School's assorted regulations. O'Malley mused that this was a touch ironic for a town most famous for the lynching of an innocent woman . . .

After reassuring Jeremy Winchester that the school would do everything in its power to hold off an embarrassing and costly lawsuit, the next person O'Malley had to face was Margaret Walsh.

He sympathized with the woman, he really did. She had lost her husband and now had to raise a moody, violent child on her own.

But that didn't change the fact that he had to expel her son.

25

"Mr. O'Malley, I understand why this may seem like—"

O'Malley cut her off. "It doesn't matter what it seems like, it matters what it is. Even if I could come up with a reason why I shouldn't expel Kyle, I can come up with ten reasons why I should—and most of them would come from the school's lawyer. Besides, Kyle has been having enough trouble since he got here. Do you really think he'd be able to continue to function even at the low level he was at before now?"

Margaret Walsh had nothing to say to that. She just looked at O'Malley pitiably. The principal wanted desperately to be able to comfort her and reassure her. He probably could have done so far more sincerely than he did Jeremy Winchester.

But years of facing up to irritated Southie parents and entrenched Boston bureaucracy had made it easy for O'Malley to harden his heart. "I'm afraid we have no choice, Mrs. Walsh." He hesitated, then decided to invoke the old when-in-doubt-try-psychobabble rule. "This isn't the first time he's acted out."

"He's been having a very hard time of it since his father's passing," Mrs. Walsh said. "He hasn't been sleeping lately."

If she was going to whip out her own psycho-babble card, O'Malley had no choice but to take the blunt route. "I sympathize with his loss, Mrs. Walsh, but it's no excuse. He *stabbed* another child. The boy's going to need stitches."

"He was *provoked!*"

O'Malley tried not to sigh. The psychobabble defense having washed out for both of them, she was now going for the old standby: it had to be the other child's fault, because *her* child would *never* do something like that.

"My son is not violent—" she continued, but O'Malley interrupted with his trump card.

"The only way for our school to avoid a lawsuit is to expel Kyle. I'm sorry."

Mrs. Walsh, unsurprisingly, had no reply. O'Malley was worried that she might try the we-can-fight-the-lawsuit argument, but either she knew better, or she had just lost the will to keep the argument going.

Given how much of a troublemaker her son had been, O'Malley suspected that she'd be having a lot of these conversations. And they'd all end the same way. It was not going to be easy, and O'Malley felt a pang of sympathy.

"If you like," he said as he got up, "I can give you a list of schools that specialize in troubled children."

Mrs. Walsh also stood. "That won't be necessary." They exited the office. Kyle was sitting on the bench outside O'Malley's office, staring straight ahead. To O'Malley's dismay, he *still* hadn't wiped the spittle off his chin, and it had now dried, making it almost look like a scar.

"Come along, Kyle," Mrs. Walsh said, holding out a hand. Kyle took it and got up from the bench.

The two of them walked toward the door to the school. O'Malley watched them and thought that it was all such a waste.

Then Kyle turned around and looked at O'Malley over his shoulder.

When he was the dean at the Southie high school, there was one boy named William McGreal. McGreal was like Kyle: sullen, not too many friends, always getting into fights. There were rumors that McGreal and one of his friends—the friend was also a Southie but enrolled in a different school—were involved in an assault on three kids, though no charges were ever filed.

One day in the cafeteria, McGreal got into an argument with one of the other kids. McGreal then took out a switchblade that he had somehow got past the metal detectors the state had required them to put in and plunged it right into the other kid's chest.

When the police came and took McGreal away, he stared at O'Malley. This was a boy of fifteen who had just taken the life of a fellow student. But O'Malley saw no remorse in his eyes, no caring, no regret. Nothing.

William McGreal's eyes were dead.

The next day, Scott O'Malley started looking for another job.

Today, O'Malley saw the same look in Kyle Walsh's eyes that he had seen in William McGreal's.

Shuddering, O'Malley broke the gaze and went back into his office, grateful for the bottle of Scotch he kept in the bottom drawer of his desk.

four

Sarah Orne was scared.

The four-year-old girl's mouth had been hurting for days now. Mother said that it was normal, but then one of her teeth started *moving*. Teeth weren't supposed to *move*.

Mother tried to explain it to her, but it didn't make any sense. Why would her teeth just fall *out* like that?

Sarah was scared that she was going to wind up like Auntie Margie. Auntie Margie didn't have any teeth, and she talked funny. Sarah did not want to be like her.

But then her older sister, Mary, explained it to her. Mary had always been better than Mother or Father at explaining things. Her parents' explanations never made any sense, but Mary's did. Mary had explained once before about the difference between rain and snow: snow came up out of the ground, where rain came from the sky; it only looked like snow fell down because of the wind. And she also explained that losing teeth was a way of not being a baby anymore.

Mary also knew a secret. You could trade your old teeth that fell out for sweets.

"Really?" Sarah said with her mouth that still hurt.

"Uh-huh. When your tooth finally comes out—and it's a *baby* tooth, so you don't want it anymore anyhow—we'll go up to the Lady of the Lighthouse, and she'll give us sweets!"

Sarah had heard about Lady Lighthouse from her friend Charlotte. Charlotte's mother told Charlotte that Lady Lighthouse used to make cakes for Charlotte's older sister Samantha's birthdays, and for Charlotte's, too, when she was one and two, but Charlotte didn't remember that because she was just a baby then.

Sarah was still just a baby, according to Mary. But she wouldn't be when her tooth came out. And then she'd be able to get Lady Lighthouse to make her a cake or a cookie or a pie or something even better!

Days passed. Sarah's mouth still hurt, and her tooth got looser. But it wouldn't come out.

One day, she even asked Mary to try to pull it out, but that hurt even more, and Sarah cried for the rest of the day. Mother spanked Mary for trying to hurt her sister, and Sarah was too busy crying to tell Mother that it wasn't Mary's fault, that Sarah had asked her.

It was a warm, sunny Sunday in June when the tooth finally came out. It was funny, because Sarah had given up on the tooth. She had decided that it would never come out and she was going to be a baby forever. Her mouth had even stopped hurting. The creepy man at church that morning had talked about how important babies were, so maybe God was telling her that she was meant to be a baby so she could always be important.

And then, when she was walking home from church with the rest of her family, it suddenly just fell out.

"My tooth!" Sarah reached down to the cobblestone and grabbed it.

"Sarah!" Mother said in that voice she always used when Sarah did something bad.

"It's okay, Mother!" Mary said. "She's gonna take the tooth to the Lady!"

"Oh, no," Mother said, still using that voice. "No, I don't want you going to that—that woman."

"But Mo-o-o-other!" Sarah cried. How could

she stop being a baby if she didn't get a sweet for her tooth?

"Edna got to go to the Tooth Lady," Mary said.

Sarah smiled, glad that her sister was helping. Mother listened to her more because she was older.

"But—"

"And so did Matthew and Lucas and Freddie and—"

Mother turned to Father. "John, please, tell them they can't go."

Father just laughed. "Oh, don't be such a fussbudget, Mildred."

"But, John, that—that woman is so—so—"

"So *what,* darling?"

"Have you ever *met* her?"

Father scratched his chin. "Can't say as I have. Met her husband once, before that awful storm. Damn shame, that. Seemed a good fellow, all things considered. Solid, Christian man. Good head on his shoulders. Thought the world of her, I can tell you that. And if Captain Dixon thought his wife was a good woman, then that's a good enough testimonial for me."

Sarah hated when adults went on like this, because she had no idea what they were talking about. She clutched the tooth in her small hand. It didn't look anything like it did when it was in her mouth. It had these weird spiky things at the end of it. Sarah wondered if growing those spiky things were why it fell out of her mouth.

"John, I swear to you, sometimes—oh!" Mother got that look on her face that she usually got whenever Sarah or Mary did something wrong. "Very well, you can go see the Tooth Lady, but only if you go before it gets dark!"

"Yay!"

Sarah started skipping her way down the road. She was going to get her sweet! She wasn't a baby anymore!

Later that afternoon, Mary and Sarah went up to Lighthouse Point. It had gotten cloudy, which Sarah didn't like, but at least they were nice fluffy clouds. Mother had wrapped Sarah's tooth in a handkerchief and tied it with a nice ribbon. "If you *must* go, you shouldn't lose the tooth," Mother had said.

Before Sarah could even see the Tooth Lady's house, she could smell the gingerbread. She and Mary had already been practically skipping, but as soon as they smelled the gingerbread, they started running.

Gingerbread was Sarah's favorite thing in the whole world.

Mother had always made good gingerbread, but

this was much, much better smelling. It was the best gingerbread Sarah had ever smelled.

She just hoped it tasted as good.

Mary had longer legs, so she made it to the front door first. Usually, this close to the water, Sarah could smell the ocean, but all she had in her nose was the gingerbread. She decided that she really liked not being a baby anymore if it meant all this gingerbread!

By the time Sarah caught up to Mary at the front door, yelling, "Wait for me, wait for me!" the whole way, the big wooden door started to open.

Sarah had been worried, after all the stories Mary had told about how the Tooth Lady was an old woman who'd lost her husband and didn't have any children, that she was going to be a crazy old lady like Auntie Margie.

Instead, the door opened to a beautiful woman. She had long blond hair that was tied back and looked as if the sun were coming out of her head.

She smiled down at the girls. "Yes?"

Sarah couldn't make her mouth work. She could talk just fine when her mouth hurt because she wasn't going to be a baby anymore, but now she couldn't say anything. The Lady was just too beautiful. She looked like the faerie, like in the stories that Grandmama used to tell her before she went to sleep at night. Didn't the faerie used to have sweet food, too?

Mary, as usual, came to her rescue. "My baby sister lost a tooth."

"I'm *not* a baby no more!" Sarah found her voice again. She held up the bundle Mother had made. "I lost my baby tooth!"

"Well, good for you," the Fairy Lady said. "It's so good to see children growing up."

The Fairy Lady sounded sad about that. "Is something wrong?" Sarah asked.

"No," the Lady said, smiling again. "Nothing at all, you dear, sweet child. You're John and Mildred Orne's girls, aren't you?"

"Yes, ma'am," Mary said.

"Why don't you come in, and I'll give you some nice gingerbread? Do you like gingerbread?"

"Oh, *yes!*" Sarah could hardly stop herself from running into the house. But she remembered how Mother always said that she shouldn't run in the house. And she should behave well in other people's houses. So she walked very slowly into the house.

The house was a lot like Sarah's house, except there weren't any toys or playthings. Mary had said that the Tooth Lady didn't have any children, so she wouldn't have any of that kind of thing, Sarah remembered.

And there were also all the white things.

They looked kind of like Sarah's tooth, only much bigger, and with pictures on them. Sarah tried to imagine someone putting a picture on her tooth.

"I like the pictures," Sarah said.

"What was that, dear?" the Lady asked.

"I said I like the pictures."

"Oh, thank you." The Lady walked over to one of them and ran her hand over it. "They're—well, thank you."

The lady seemed sad again. Sarah was scared that the Fairy Lady wouldn't like her anymore and not give her gingerbread. "I'm sorry, Fairy Lady."

To Sarah's surprise, that brought the Lady's smile back. "What did you call me?"

"Don't pay her any heed, ma'am," Mary said. Sarah thought she sounded just like Mother. "She thinks you're a fairy. Just like a *baby* would think."

"I'm *not* a baby!"

"Of course you're not, dear," the Fairy Lady said. "Come along, let's go to the kitchen and get you some of that gingerbread."

"Yay!"

It was the best gingerbread Sarah had ever had.

For the rest of the week, Sarah told everyone who'd listen—and plenty of people who wouldn't— about how she went to the Fairy Tooth Lady and had the best treats and she wasn't a baby anymore because she lost her baby tooth.

Mother kept saying what a bad idea it had been to let Sarah go up there, but Sarah just thought Mother was mad because Sarah didn't like Mother's gingerbread as much as the Fairy Tooth Lady's.

The happiest day of Sarah's four-year-old life was when her mouth started hurting again. She did everything she could to force the tooth to come out sooner, especially when she found out that the Fairy Tooth Lady might be baking a Queen cake . . .

five

1990

Kyle Walsh really hated it when his mother tucked him in. It made him feel like a baby.

Still, he let her do it because he knew it made her happy. And today, especially, after what he did, he wanted to do whatever he could to make her happy.

Every time he closed his eyes, he saw the blood.

Sometimes it was his blood in the boys' room. Sometimes it was Ray's blood. Sometimes it was just blood, flowing like a river.

What scared Kyle the most was that these constant images of blood *didn't* scare him.

Going to bed, though, that scared him. Going to bed hadn't been a good thing in a very long time.

Mom looked down at him as she pulled the blanket up to his neck. "I know things have been hard since your father left."

Kyle rolled his eyes. He hated when Mom got like this. "Dad didn't leave, he *died.*"

As usual when this subject came up, Mom changed it. "Why'd you hurt that boy?"

"I don't know," Kyle muttered, looking away. The sad thing was, it was the total truth. Looking back on it, he really didn't know why he had stabbed Ray. Sure, Ray was a jerk, but Ray had *always* been a jerk. That didn't mean he deserved to be stabbed. Made fun of, sure. Maybe even beat up. But not *stabbed.* That was nuts.

And so Kyle wondered if *he* was nuts.

"Kyle, look at me," Mom said.

Kyle did so.

"Why?"

"I really don't know. I wish I hadn't, though." He took a breath. "Mom? What's wrong with me?"

Grabbing Kyle in a hug, Mom said, "Nothing's wrong with you, baby."

The hug made Kyle feel better. Unfortunately, better wasn't the same as good. "Then why do I keep having those dreams?"

"The doctor said sometimes they just happen to people."

Mom had been saying that all week. "But why *me?* It's almost every night now." For the first time all day, he let himself actually remember the dreams—the nightmares—he'd been having, and he shivered under the blanket. "I don't want to hurt anyone."

"I know you don't, baby."

Of course, it was easy for Mom to say that. *She* knew he didn't want to hurt anyone, that he didn't want to do those things he did in his dreams.

But nobody else knew it. And obviously, since they had expelled him from school today, nobody else really cared, either.

Mom took Kyle's hand in hers. "I'll make you a promise. Whatever's going on with you, we'll figure it out together, okay?"

Kyle was about to say that it wasn't as if they had a choice, but he didn't say that. That wasn't fair to Mom. This was hard on her, too, especially on top of Dad dying and all.

"Okay," he said. He even managed to smile.

So did she. "Now get some sleep." She got up, gave him a final smile, turned out the light, and left.

Kyle sat alone for a while, staring at the ceiling. He certainly had no interest in going to sleep. The room was dark, lit only by a clown night-light that he'd had for as long as he could remember. Kyle had never liked total darkness, and he liked it even less lately. Shadows could be scary, but total darkness was a lot worse.

He waited until he was sure he heard his mother close the door to her room—she always went to bed at the same time he did, even though she was a grown-up and could stay up later if she wanted to—then got up and went to the hamper. Reaching in, he felt around for the pants he had worn today and then into the front right pocket.

At some point when he was sitting on that stupid bench outside Principal O'Malley's office, Kyle's last baby tooth had finally fallen out. It had been kind of a relief, really. For one thing, it gave him something to do: he sucked all the blood down into his throat, since he wasn't about to be allowed to go to the bathroom.

Besides, then he'd *see* the blood. A part of him desperately wanted to see the blood. Another part wanted to throw up at the very idea. Since the part that wanted to see it was also the part that wanted to stab Ray, Kyle figured it was best not to give that part of him any help.

He wasn't sure why he had kept the tooth. Probably, he just didn't know what to do with it. So he had shoved it into his pocket.

Now he didn't want anything to do with it.

Maybe if it hadn't come loose like it did, he wouldn't have been bleeding in the bathroom that morning, and maybe he wouldn't have gone all crazy staring at the blood, and maybe he wouldn't have stabbed Ray, and maybe he wouldn't be expelled.

Kyle threw the tooth onto the floor and headed back to the bed.

He was startled by a scratching noise.

Stopping dead in his tracks, Kyle gazed around the room.

The sound had come from the window.

Slowly, very slowly, Kyle walked toward the window.

He pushed aside the drapes but saw nothing there. He opened the glass, which let the cool night air in. Shivering a bit from a breeze, he stuck his head out.

Figuring he probably had just imagined it, he was about to go back inside and close the window when a huge face suddenly appeared out of nowhere and cried, *"Boo!"*

Startled, Kyle jumped, almost hitting his head on the windowpane.

His heart beating like crazy, he thought for sure that some kind of creature—*like the thing in his dreams*—was going to kill him, and he almost screamed himself.

Then he got a good look at the face, which was *not* huge; it just looked it because it was so close. Though it did belong to someone who, despite being the same age and being a girl, was bigger than Kyle.

It was Cat Greene.

Whose arms were pinwheeling, as Kyle's startled jump had knocked her off balance, and she was about to fall into Mom's privet bush.

"Damn!"

He reached out and grabbed her arm, which kept her from falling, and she clambered into his room.

They stared at each other for a minute. Cat was breathing heavy, probably because she almost fell. Kyle was breathing heavy, too, mainly because he'd been scared. His heart was still beating like crazy.

"That was stupid," he said to her.

She grinned. "Yeah, you're probably right. How are you?"

"Okay, I guess," he lied. "How's Ray?" He asked out of habit more than anything else. He honestly didn't care much how Ray was, as long as he wasn't dead.

"He's gonna need stitches. He's a dick, anyway."

"Yeah." Kyle stared at Cat. He didn't get what she was doing there. "Why aren't you scared of me like everyone else?"

Giving him a look, Cat said, "I weigh, like, twenty pounds more than you. You ever tried that on me, I'd kick your ass."

Kyle laughed at that, and so did she. It was the first real laugh Kyle had had in a long time. In fact, Kyle couldn't remember the last time he had laughed for real. Not the laughter he felt building up in him in the bathroom when he stared at the blood or in class when Kimberly was making a jerk of herself or when he stabbed Ray. *Real* laughing at something that was *really* funny.

"I heard they kicked you out," Cat said after a second.

"They all think I'm crazy."

She looked down and noticed the tooth, the light from the clown night-light shining right on it. "You *are* crazy, throwing this away. This one's special." She picked it up. Kyle couldn't imagine why.

"Special?"

"Your last baby tooth." She smiled. "Means you're not a baby anymore."

Kyle smiled, mainly because he had been thinking the exact same thing, though he still didn't see why it was worth saving the stupid tooth. It wasn't as if the tooth fairy was *real* or anything. She *was* real back in 18-whatever-it-was, but they killed her.

Just like they killed Dad.

Suddenly, Cat leaned forward and kissed Kyle.

Kyle had seen people kiss before, of course. Mostly on TV and in movies and stuff. He'd seen Mom and Dad kiss lots of times, too, before Dad died. It was something he probably knew that he'd do someday, but since most girls were stupid, he didn't think it'd be any time soon. At least, not as long as he lived in this town. The idea of him kissing somebody like Kimberly or any of her friends was just nuts.

Cat had always been different, though. Cat wasn't afraid of anything or anyone, and she wasn't stupid. In fact, Kyle sometimes thought she was the only person besides him who wasn't in the whole town.

But he'd never thought about kissing her before.

In fact, he'd never really thought about kissing anyone. He had no idea what it was supposed to feel like.

Now that it had happened, now that he had felt her cold lips touch his warm ones, he thought that it wasn't all that bad.

She broke off the kiss and stared at him. "Tastes like metal."

"Sorry," Kyle said, feeling as if he'd let her down somehow. She didn't taste like metal. He didn't know what she tasted like, only that it was like nothing Kyle had ever tasted before.

All he'd been tasting today, of course, was the salty taste of his own blood . . .

She turned back to the window. "Wait," he said quickly, not wanting her to go.

Stopping, she turned and looked at him with That Look again.

"It's just, I—"

Before he could go on, she kissed him again.

He finally figured it out: golden raspberries. Not that Cat's lips tasted anything like fruit, but he remembered the time he visited Uncle John in upstate New York, and he had a whole bunch of fruit growing in his backyard, including golden raspberries. They looked like normal, red raspberries, except they were a golden color, and they tasted *so* much better than the red ones. Kyle had thought the golden raspberries were the best thing he'd ever tasted.

He had that same feeling from Cat's second kiss.

"What was that for?" he asked in a whisper.

"First time shouldn't taste like blood. Should be sweet."

Golden raspberries, Kyle recalled, were very sweet.

Cat put the tooth under Kyle's pillow. Then she climbed up onto the windowsill.

"Don't forget, when the Tooth Fairy comes— don't peek."

Kyle followed her to the window and once again leaned out. This time, Cat's face didn't startle him out of nowhere. Instead, she tightrope-walked over to the trellis, then climbed down and ran off toward her own house.

It didn't feel so cold anymore.

Not even bothering to close the window, Kyle climbed back into bed. The sheets, which had felt almost smothering before, now comforted him. He reached under the pillow and felt his last baby tooth.

Means you're not a baby anymore.

He wasn't a baby anyway. Babies didn't have dreams like he did. Babies didn't stab people.

Babies didn't kiss pretty girls.

Kyle had never thought of Cat as pretty before tonight. He wondered how he could have missed that about her.

He faded off to sleep, comforted by the presence of the tooth under his pillow, not because he expected some stupid Tooth Fairy to show up and take it away in exchange for a quarter, but because Cat had put it there.

The last thing he saw before he went to sleep was the curtains blowing in the night's breeze.

For once, he didn't dream.

He was, however, awakened by a buzzing noise.

His eyes flew open. He looked around the room.

The curtains still flapped in the breeze.

The clown night-light continued to cast its shadows.

But something about the shadows looked different.

Like monsters.

But only babies saw monsters in the dark.

And Kyle wasn't a baby anymore.

He closed his eyes, forcing himself to go back to sleep and not be stupid.

A minute later, he opened his eyes again.

He still heard the noise. He had no idea what the noise was, but it would not go away.

Looking up at the lamp next to his bed, he debated turning it on.

No. That was what a baby would do.

He closed his eyes again, pulling the covers up tight around his neck.

The noises would not stop.

Then the night-light went out.

Bereft of the red-and-white light coming from the clown face, Kyle's bedroom was plunged into darkness.

No darkness! There has to be some light!

He fumbled for the lamp and switched it on. The darkness went away, eaten up by the bright light of the lamp.

Everything in Kyle's room was right where he'd left it. His desk, his hamper, his posters, his comic books, his action figures, his school stuff, all of it. He reached under the pillow, and his tooth was still there. Everything was fine.

He got up and went over to the clown night-light and jiggled it in the wall socket. It came back on, the smiling face with its wide eyes and bright red lips—

(Lips the same color as the blood in your mouth and on Ray's back.)

—shining brightly. It had just come loose. No big deal.

Only babies were afraid of the dark.

So why wouldn't he turn the light back out?

There was something in the room with him. Kyle just *knew* it.

(The same way you knew you had to stab Ray?)

If he turned the light back out, whatever it was would come out.

Kids always thought monsters came out only in the dark. Maybe they did, maybe they didn't, but right now, Kyle wasn't taking the chance.

The house had one bathroom on the second floor, which had doors to both bedrooms. Kyle went into the bathroom and saw that Mom had left her bathroom door open. He looked into her room.

She was sleeping soundly, tucked into her bed as snug as Kyle had been before Cat's appearance woke him up.

He wouldn't wake her. Not until he was sure.

Looking around the bathroom, his eyes settled on the scissors Mom kept on the sink. They were perfect.

(Just like the protractor was for Ray.)

Grabbing the scissors in his hand, holding them over his head, point downward, he went back to his bedroom, ready to face whatever was there.

Margaret Walsh dreamed of her husband.

She knew that her son was in his bed, dreaming of something more horrible. They'd gone to doctors, to guidance counselors, but nothing seemed to help him get over the night terrors.

Margaret was scared for her son.

And she missed her husband.

She wondered how Kyle would grow up. Would he be plagued by these dreams all his life, or would they fade as he got older? Would he start finally having friends? Would he go through puberty like any normal boy and start dating girls and roughhousing and doing all the other things boys did? Or would he stay sullen and moody and difficult?

Would he continue to have these odd violent episodes?

And would he keep having that dead look in his eyes that he'd had when she picked him up at school? She almost hadn't recognized the near-zombie sitting outside the principal's office that afternoon. It was a huge relief to see Kyle's eyes back to normal—*alive* again—tonight.

Margaret didn't know what the future was going to bring. The thought scared her. She knew that motherhood didn't come with an instruction manual, but it *was* supposed to come with a support staff: the father. She didn't have that, either.

Now she needed to find a new school for Kyle. Maybe a new town. True, they had family here, but maybe it was time to start over completely.

She missed her husband.

In her dream, the two of them were walking along the coast of Darkness Falls, approaching the lighthouse. The moon was full, and they were holding hands. She could feel the sand between her toes as they walked, but, oddly, she couldn't feel her husband's hand, even though she clasped it tightly.

They stopped walking, in the dream, and stared into each other's eyes. He had such beautiful hazel eyes.

They kissed. Margaret thought the kiss tasted metallic.

Somebody screamed.

Margaret jumped awake, almost strangling herself with her covers.

Kyle. Kyle was screaming.

She disentangled herself from her bedsheets and ran to the bathroom that adjoined her bedroom and Kyle's.

He wasn't there, nor was he in his bedroom, though the light was on in the latter.

She ran out into the hallway, scared that something—something *else*—had happened to her son. Margaret wasn't sure how much more of this she could take. First Kyle's father dying, then Kyle's dreams, then his *stabbing* people . . .

Taking a deep breath, Margaret pulled herself together. He was somewhere in the house, he had to be. He probably just had another bad dream.

As she passed the hallway entrance to the bathroom, she heard a sound. She whipped her head around and saw her reflection in the mirror.

She also saw something in the shadows behind her.

Then she heard the noise again. She whirled around to see that it was just the clothes on the hallway hanger, rustling in the breeze.

Except there was no breeze out here.

"Kyle?"

The next thing she knew, a sharp object impaled her stomach, blood spurting out all over the place.

Oddly, the first thing she thought was that it would take forever to get the stains out of the hall carpet.

The last thing she thought was that the kiss with her husband in her dream shouldn't have tasted so metallic . . .

Caitlin Greene didn't understand what had happened.

She stood on the front porch with her mother and her infant brother, Michael. The flickering red-and-white lights of the ambulance lit up the street with odd colors and shadows. It was kind of like a strobe-light version of the way Kyle's clown light lit up his room.

Kyle . . .

Caitlin had *just* seen him. He was *fine*.

Okay, sure, he hadn't been sleeping much lately, but why should that matter? That was why she had gone by to visit him in the first place, because she knew he'd been having a hard time sleeping.

She had even *kissed* him, for God's sake!

She still wasn't sure why she had done that. Kyle just seemed so much cooler than the other people in town. Everyone else was so caught up in their silly cliques or whatever—it was all just so phony.

But Kyle had never been phony. She really liked that.

So why did he turn out to be a killer?

No. Caitlin refused to believe it. She just *saw* him. There was *no way* that Kyle could have killed his own *mother.*

And yet there was Officer Henry putting a tag on a bag that held a bloody pair of scissors. And Mrs. Walsh being put in a bag by the paramedics. And Kyle sitting, wrapped in a blanket that one of the cops had given him, looking just as dead as his mother, in total shock.

Just as he did when he stabbed Ray.

Half the town was gathered nearby, of course. It's not as if anything as interesting as a boy stabbing his mother the same day he stabbed a classmate usually happened in this town. Hell, it was probably the most exciting thing to happen around here since they lynched the Tooth Fairy . . .

Caitlin could hear the mutterings from the grown-ups. "He was in class with my daughter." "Spooky kid." "I always thought there was something, y'know, *wrong* with him." "That poor woman, to have to live alone with *that.*"

Then another voice sounded over the noise of people kicking Kyle while he was down and over the cops talking to one another.

57

"Let me through! This is my aunt's house! What hap—"

The voice cut itself off just as the person it belonged to came into view. It was Kyle's cousin, Larry.

One of the cops—Caitlin couldn't tell who it was from this far off—started talking to Larry in a quiet voice. Meanwhile, Officer Henry walked over to Kyle with some old lady who reminded Caitlin of the school's icky guidance counselor.

Caitlin hated guidance counselors. So did Kyle.

"Kyle, this is Dr. Jenkins," the officer said.

Dr. Jenkins didn't actually say anything, she just guided Kyle by the shoulder toward a van that said "County Social Services" on the door.

Caitlin realized that they were going to take Kyle away. Probably forever.

Stupidly, the first thing she thought was that Kyle never got his money from the Tooth Fairy.

Then again, what more natural thing to think in *this* town?

Idly, she fingered the charm necklace that she always wore. Her mother had given it to her when her little brother, Michael, was born—a kind of consolation prize, a way to reassure her that they still loved her even though they had a new baby.

All of a sudden, Caitlin came to a decision.

58

Looking up, she saw her mother staring ahead, rocking Michael in his blue blanket.

Then Caitlin unhooked the smiling sun charm from the necklace and, before her mother could stop her, ran out toward Kyle.

She got to the van just as Kyle took his seat in the first passenger bench right behind the driver. He still looked all dazed and confused, but he did actually turn his head to look at Caitlin.

Grabbing his hand, Caitlin put the sun charm on top of his palm and closed his fingers over it. She even smiled at him.

Kyle didn't return the smile.

Dr. Jenkins gently pushed Caitlin aside so she could slide the door to the van shut. Then the older woman got into the shotgun seat, and the van drove off.

Caitlin wondered if Kyle would ever smile again.

six

1840

Sam Smith thought going to the Tooth Fairy's house was a bad idea.

It was one thing if they actually had any teeth to offer her. All the children of Darkness Falls knew that if you went to the weird lady up at Lighthouse Point with one of your baby teeth, you'd get sweets in return.

But neither Sam nor his best friend, Thomas, *had* any teeth.

What they had was hunger. After all, it was *hours* until supper, and they'd been playing all day. Neither Sam's mother nor Thomas's would let them have anything to spoil their appetites. "Dessert comes *after* the meal," Mama had always said.

Thomas, though, wanted treats *now,* and he knew that the Tooth Fairy would be baking something.

"How do you know that?" Sam had asked.

Rolling his eyes, Thomas said, "Because she's *always* baking something."

Sam then punched Thomas in the arm.

But up to Lighthouse Point they went. Or, rather, Thomas went and Sam reluctantly followed.

"Are you *sure* this is a good idea?"

"Why shouldn't it be?"

"My papa says—"

Again, Thomas rolled his eyes. "Your papa says that mermaids ate all the fish in the Atlantic Ocean last year."

"How do you know they didn't?" Sam asked defiantly. "Anyway, Papa says that the Tooth Fairy is a crazy old witch woman and that she eats children who don't bring her teeth."

They were almost at the house now. Sam could smell the honey and the baking bread.

"She is *not* a witch woman. Sarah saw her when *she* lost her first baby tooth and said she was beautiful."

"So?"

"So, oaf, witch women aren't beautiful. They're ugly and warty. *Everyone* knows that."

Sam stuck his tongue out at Thomas. "Sarah Orne's just a girl. What does *she* know about anything?"

"But you believe your papa about mermaids?"

"I didn't say that!" Sam was feeling defensive now. He wanted to go back home. He didn't like the sound of the waves beating against the rock the lighthouse was on, didn't like having to run uphill to the house.

However, he did like the smells that were coming from the house. His mouth started watering, his stomach grumbling. Suddenly, the time until supper seemed like forever.

Now that they were almost at the house, Thomas put his finger to his lips, and they stopped running and started tiptoeing.

One of the windows was open. Crouching low so that the Tooth Fairy couldn't see them, Sam and Thomas dashed to the space under the window. Thomas then slowly poked his head above the windowsill so he could see inside.

Sam whispered, "Do you see any—"

Thomas crouched back down, out of sight of anyone inside, and gave Sam a stern look. "Shhh!" he whispered back. "Your stomach makes enough noise."

Self-consciously, Sam put his hands over his stomach. He couldn't help it. The house smelled *so* good.

"She's made crullers with honey," Thomas said with a smile.

Sam had to wipe his lips. Those were his favorite, and Thomas knew it.

Again, Thomas poked his head up. Then he looked down. "She's leaving the room," he whispered. "Come on."

Thomas clambered up onto the windowsill as he spoke. Sam got out of his crouch and did the same.

It was, of course, unbearably hot in the kitchen. The stove had been going full bore, after all. That was probably why the Tooth Fairy had left the kitchen, so she could cool down.

Which left the place free for Sam and Thomas to raid the crullers, since they didn't have the usual payment.

Thomas headed straight for the crullers, of course, and Sam was about to follow, when something caught his eye.

It didn't make sense. It was *so* hot in the kitchen that they needed to grab their treats and get out as quickly as possible.

But there was this urn on the shelf . . .

Most of what was on the shelf consisted of pots, pans, and other dishware. But sitting in the middle of it all was a large green urn.

Thomas was grabbing a cruller with one hand and stuffing another one into his mouth with the other hand. "Hurry up, Sam," he said, though it sounded more like "Hermy mmp, Sum" with his mouth full of baked bread and honey.

Sam, though, was captivated by the green urn, which stood out so much from the wood of the kitchen—blackened from so much exposure to the heat and flames of the stove—and the dark cookware. It wasn't in the cupboard with the other containers or in the scullery with the supplies.

He found that he *had* to know what was in it.

"Sam!" Thomas urged, having swallowed his first cruller, the second poised to go into his mouth at a moment's notice.

"Hang on, Thomas, I just want to see something."

The shelf was just in Sam's reach if he stood on the tips of his toes. His small fingers brushed against the green urn, and it started to topple. As it fell forward, he was able to grab it with both hands.

Then he lost his balance.

He tried to straighten himself out and still hold on to the urn, but he needed both hands for that, so he couldn't balance himself, nor could he hold on to anything. So he let go of the urn and flailed his arms.

It didn't work, and he went crashing down to the kitchen floor.

So did about half the cookware, which made a horrible racket.

Sam was so scared that the Tooth Fairy would

hear the noise that he didn't even think about what the falling cookware might do.

Thomas yelled at him, no longer really worried that he might be heard, all things considered. "Sam, you stupid oaf, watch out for—"

Several pots clattered to the floor. One or two of them hit the small door to the stove. The stove, which still had embers burning from the baking, sparked, and some of the wood shifted as the pots knocked the door open.

"—the stove," Thomas finished just as some of those embers arced across the kitchen and hit the wood shelves.

It didn't take very long after that for the kitchen to catch fire. Especially since Sam and Thomas just sat there amidst the fallen cookware with their mouths hanging open, waiting for—

What?

Once the fire started seriously going, Sam got up and ran for the window, Thomas right behind him. What had already been a steaming hot kitchen became a roaring inferno, and Sam was convinced that his skeleton was going to catch fire, it was so hot.

Thomas reached the window first and climbed up to the sill. As Sam waited to climb up after him—convinced that his pants would catch fire and that he'd die right there and go to hell for stealing even though he didn't actually steal anything—he turned around.

Expecting to see only more fire, he was surprised to see a woman standing in the middle of the flames. Her blond hair glowed in the firelight.

It was at once the most beautiful and the most frightening sight Sam Smith had ever seen.

She was clutching the green urn in one arm, the other arm making sure the lid was secure.

"Don't peek."

Sam shouldn't have been able to hear her. The fire was getting very loud, competing also with the sound of the waves crashing into the lighthouse. Plus, Sam's own heart was beating so fast he was sure they could hear it in Boston town. And the Tooth Fairy—for that was who the blond woman had to be—hadn't spoken very loudly.

But Sam heard her clearly.

Thomas was already running down the path. Sam wiped the prodigious amounts of sweat from his brow and climbed up onto the sill. His sweaty hands slipped on the sill, and he almost fell to the floor again, but this time he managed to right himself.

As he and Thomas ran down the path away from Lighthouse Point, the cool sea air feeling so refreshing, Sam cried out, "I *told* you coming here was a bad idea!"

seven

2002

Caitlin Greene hated the smell of hospitals.

She had grown up with the tangy, salty air quality of living by the sea in Darkness Falls. The antiseptic odor of the typical hospital corridor had always felt wrong to her.

So naturally, she had been spending far too much time in hospitals lately.

She hadn't even realized that she'd been tuning out the doctor—the latest in a series—until he repeated her name three times.

"Sorry," she muttered.

The doctor, a nice bespectacled man in his fifties named Murphy, continued with the diagnosis regarding her brother, Michael, as they walked down the corridor toward his room. Caitlin had heard so many doctors talk about Michael at this point that she could recite his words before he did.

"As I was saying, noctiphobia is very common in his age group. We've run one CAT scan and two MRIs at your behest, and the conclusions all say the same thing: there's nothing wrong with your brother."

Which is exactly what Caitlin had expected him to say. As if the tests were more right than what she'd been *seeing* with her own eyes.

She tried to hold in her temper as she said, "My brother has not been able to sleep for more than ten minutes at a time for the last six months. *You* go tell him there's nothing wrong with him."

Dr. Murphy stopped walking and sighed. Caitlin also stopped and fixed him with an expectant glare.

"I meant there's nothing *physically* wrong. Ms. Greene, we've run every test possible. There's nothing more we can do—"

Murphy was interrupted by a scream coming from a room down the hall.

Caitlin's legs were off and running before her conscious mind even registered why: that was Michael's scream.

God knew she'd heard it enough times over the last six months.

The door to his room was open, so Caitlin was able to dash in at a dead run, to see Michael, wide awake and freaking out as if someone were coming after him with a knife.

But the only other person in his hospital room was a nurse, whose eyes were as wide as saucers.

"What happened?" Caitlin asked.

"He was asleep," the nurse stammered. "I just shut off the light by the window—"

"Don't let her shut off any lights!"

It was all Caitlin could do to hold in a curse. Didn't these stupid nurses *read* the charts? She had specifically said when they checked Michael in that there always had to be a light on in the room no matter what. Caitlin had seen Dr. Murphy mark it on the chart and everything.

She walked over to Michael and embraced him as best she could with him in the hospital bed. "It's okay, Mikey, it's all right now."

Michael was shuddering in Caitlin's arms as he spoke. "Please don't let them shut them off."

"I won't," Caitlin said. "We'll leave all the lights on. Just try and sleep."

She spent several more seconds soothing and calming him until he finally came out of the embrace and lay back down. His eyes, bloodshot from months of inadequate sleep, finally closed, his

71

thin arms drawing the heavily starched hospital sheets up to his neck, his mouth hanging open, showing the gap where he'd lost a baby tooth.

After giving a final glare to the nurse, Caitlin went back out into the hallway. Murphy had a quick whispered exchange with the nurse—Caitlin hoped it was a reprimand of some kind—before rejoining her.

"Isn't there something else you can check on?" she asked plaintively.

"No. He is a twelve-year-old boy who is afraid of the dark, and that's all."

God, he made it sound so—so—*mundane.* Caitlin was about halfway between punching Murphy out and breaking down and crying.

Just when she thought she'd do both at the same time, Murphy's face softened.

"Look, I'm not saying your brother doesn't have a problem—"

Caitlin had to bite her tongue to stop herself from remarking snidely, *Gee, how generous of you to acknowledge that.*

"—but whatever it is, it's psychosomatic. My advice would be for you to get a second opinion."

Refraining from pointing out that Murphy was around her fourteenth opinion, she instead just said, "From *where*?"

"From someone who's more experienced in this field. Someone who's dealt with it before."

"And where am I—"

Caitlin cut herself off.

She thought about the gap in Michael's mouth where his most recent baby tooth had fallen out.

And she remembered someone else who had been having trouble sleeping.

More to the point, she remembered what had happened next.

He had lost a baby tooth, too.

"I think I know just who to call," she told Dr. Murphy, and then walked off before he could ask who.

She went out to the waiting area, where Larry Fleishman was sitting reading the paper.

At her approach, Larry put the paper down, pushed his glasses up his nose, and started to ask, "What did the doc—"

"Do you know where your cousin Kyle is?"

Larry blinked. "Kyle? What does *he* have to do with—"

"I think Michael's going through the same thing Kyle did."

"Michael—" Larry hesitated. Then he spoke very gently. "Michael hasn't killed anyone."

Caitlin winced. "I know, but—maybe he can help

Michael get through it. The doctor just said that we should try talking to somebody who's dealt with it before. Kyle certainly has."

Larry stood up. "Maybe, but look, this isn't *Silence of the Lambs.* We're not gonna get insight into one nutcase by talking to anoth—"

The explosion that Caitlin had held in check while talking to Murphy finally let loose. "Michael's *not* a nutcase! And neither is Kyle!"

"I'm sorry." Larry had the good grace to be abashed. "That was a stupid thing to say, I'm *really* sorry, but—" He let out a long breath. "Look, I don't even know where Kyle is. Last I heard, he was in Vegas, but—"

Without another word, Caitlin headed to the nearest pay phone. As she dialed information, Larry walked up beside her.

After James Earl Jones thanked her for using national 411, the irritating Verizon computerized voice asked her for a city. "Las Vegas." After being asked for a listing, she said, "Walsh, first name Kyle."

The chirpy Verizon computer told her to wait one moment. Caitlin reached into her purse to pull out a pen but could find nothing to write on. She turned to Larry. "You have a piece of paper or something?"

Larry was still holding his newspaper, and he handed it over to her. "C'mon, Caitlin, you *really* think that Kyle's just going to list his number—"

He cut himself off when she started writing down a phone number, starting with 702. Admittedly, *Kyle Walsh* was a common enough name, and there could have been more than one of them in Vegas, but it was worth a shot.

Caitlin didn't want to call around Darkness Falls and stir up old ghosts if she could just find him the old-fashioned way . . .

She dialed the toll-free number that would charge the call to her calling card, then dialed the 702 number, followed by her own card number and PIN.

After three rings, a male voice said, very tentatively, "Hello?"

"Kyle?" It didn't sound exactly like him, but it *had* been twelve years. "Is this Kyle Walsh's number? This is Caitlin Greene."

There was a pause. Then: "That's not funny." The tone of the person on the other side had gone from bewildered to angry.

Which meant it had to be Kyle. Unless there was another person living in Vegas with that name who had some kind of history with someone named Caitlin Greene. She supposed that it was possible, but she'd spent the last six months growing more and more pessimistic, so she was damn well going to give optimism a shot.

"Kyle, it's Cat."

Another pause. "Caitlin?" This time, the voice was plaintive.

And it sounded just like a ten-year-old boy Caitlin knew once.

"I know, it's been a long time, but—where are my manners, how *are* you?" The words just fell out of her mouth. She had no idea what to say to Kyle now after so long, even though she was the one who had called him.

"Fine." The angry, belligerent tone had returned. "What do you want?"

Caitlin blew out a breath. Right to business. No small talk. No bullshit.

That was what Caitlin had always liked about Kyle in the first place.

"My little brother, Michael, uh—he's in the hospital. He's really scaring me. He won't sleep, not even ten minutes at a time. He won't let us shut off any lights. The doctors say he's got something called niktophobia—"

"Noctiphobia," Kyle corrected. "Night terrors."

"But they don't know how to treat him," Caitlin continued, not really interested in how the damn thing was pronounced. "I remembered that that's what they said you had, when . . ."

She trailed off. Finishing the sentence with *when*

you killed your mother was probably not the best way to get Kyle to give her a hand, after all.

When Kyle didn't say anything, she went on. "I thought you could tell me how you got over it."

Yet another pause.

"I'm sorry," was all he said before he hung up on her.

The dial tone blared in Caitlin's ear for several seconds before she finally took the phone away from her head. She stared at it, as if it somehow could explain why Kyle wouldn't help her.

But there likely would never be an explanation. After all, twelve years *was* a long time. Who knew how much Kyle had changed?

Besides, would he really *want* to be reminded of his rather unpleasant past in Darkness Falls?

He had moved to Las Vegas. Maybe he'd rebuilt his life, moved on.

"What did you expect?" Larry asked gently.

"Larry, please," Caitlin said, not wanting to get into another argument.

"We don't need him. We'll get through this."

Larry had been saying "We'll get through this" for the last several months. It was starting to ring hollow.

He put what he probably thought was a comforting arm around her shoulder, but to Caitlin it just felt like dead weight.

"Look, I wish he'd said yes, too," Larry said earnestly. "Honestly, I'd love to see the son of a bitch. But we can't make him come if he doesn't want to."

Caitlin gently removed Larry's arm. "I suppose."

Kyle Walsh liked Las Vegas because it was in the middle of the desert.

No boats. No water.

It was pretty much the diametric opposite of Darkness Falls.

Where Darkness Falls's homes were all built before the existence of the United States, most of Vegas's were built after 1950.

In Darkness Falls, everybody knew you. In Vegas, not only did nobody know you, nobody cared.

Darkness Falls got dark at night. It never got dark in Vegas.

Kyle didn't like it dark.

He looked around his small studio apartment. It was barely bigger than his bedroom as a kid in Darkness Falls. The front door had six bolt locks, and he'd had to restrain himself from installing a seventh. Bars sat dolefully in front of the windows, giving him a convict's-eye view of the brightly lit city. He had put police floodlights that cast no shadows into the ceiling.

Not that they illuminated much. His furnishings

consisted of a mattress and a bureau. The apartment would be almost totally bare but for the kitchenette.

Sitting on the bureau were six bottles full of prescription medication that he'd been taking for so long he could no longer remember a time when his morning ritual didn't include those damn pills.

No, that wasn't true. He could remember. He just chose not to. Those were not times he wished to relive.

So naturally, fate decided to intervene and make him relive them anyhow by having Cat Greene call him out of the blue.

He reached under his shirt and pulled out the necklace that he'd worn every day since he was ten.

The one with the sun charm on it.

He looked over at the bureau with the meds and at the door with the dead bolts and up at the lights that cast an almost biblical light upon the apartment, and then he looked back down at the charm.

He thought about a kiss that tasted oddly metallic.

And he thought about a little kid named Michael whom he'd last seen as an infant. Cat seemed to think that the kid was going through what Kyle had gone through.

Kyle wouldn't wish that on his worst enemy, much less the little brother of a childhood friend.

First, he'd need to call in sick to the casino. Mac-

Dougan would probably fire him, but that wouldn't even be a hardship at this point. It had taken all of Kyle's self-control—not something he had in any great supply to begin with—to keep from pummeling MacDougan every time he went to work.

Then he'd get a plane ticket. He'd saved up more than enough, even for an overpriced last-minute ticket.

Then, for the first time in more than a decade, he'd go home.

eight

The sign on the door read "Michael Greene—No Visitors."

Kyle walked right in as if he owned the place.

The plane ride to Logan Airport had been fairly uneventful once he actually got on the plane. Prior to that, of course, he had to deal with two separate random bag checks, not to mention a virtual strip search at the metal detector. Kyle was pretty sure he fit somebody's profile of a suspected terrorist, so none of it came as any surprise.

After that, though, it was clear flying for five hours across the country, followed by a train ride from Logan to South Station in Boston, an Amtrak jaunt from there to Richfield, and a cab ride from there to Darkness Falls.

He went straight to the hospital from the train station, just as the sun started to go down.

Why wait? Especially since the alternative was to start wandering around Darkness Falls looking for a bed-and-breakfast or somewhere to stay the night. He didn't want to deal with that. Didn't want to deal with Darkness Falls at all, even though that was sort of why he had come back in the first place.

No, it was better to do what he had come here to do. So he went straight to the hospital.

It had been easy enough to find his way to Michael's room. Kyle hadn't shaved, was heavily medicated, and generally looked like hammered shit, so nobody gave him a second glance in a hospital.

The hospital room's sole occupant was lying in the bed, asleep. As he gently placed his overnight bag on the floor, Kyle noted that the lights in the room were still on, even though it had long since gotten dark. There was also an irritating buzzing sound in the room, as if a fluorescent bulb had come loose.

As soon as Kyle came in, though, Michael woke up and pulled the covers up to his chin. Kyle almost smiled at that. He remembered hearing an old Bill Cosby routine from the sixties about how there was something magical about covers that monsters couldn't get at you as long as you stayed under them.

If only that were true . . .

For lack of anything better to say, Kyle said, "You must be Michael."

In response, Michael drew the covers up closer to his lower lip.

Kyle sighed. Nobody had said this would be easy.

"It's okay," he said. "I'm not gonna hurt you. I just want to talk a little. My name's Kyle."

He extended a hand. Michael tried to get further under the covers. Kyle withdrew the hand.

"Your sister says you're afraid of the dark. Makes it tough to sleep. You get a lot of sleep?"

Michael shook his head no. Kyle considered this a major breakthrough.

"Me neither."

Then Michael turned away from Kyle and started staring at the far wall. Kyle recognized the move, having practiced it many times himself: Michael had lost interest in the discussion and wanted the annoying grown-up to go the hell away.

"Maybe this wasn't such a good idea," he muttered.

The buzzing, a mild annoyance when Kyle had come in, was now driving him nuts. Or maybe he just needed a distraction. In any case, it was the work of a moment to trace the sound to the bulb over the in-room sink right next to the door to the bathroom. Kyle walked over to it, reached up, tightened it, and the buzzing stopped. The bulb also burned brighter now, shining down on the metal and ceramic of the sink.

Kyle had had a lot of practice with lightbulbs over the years . . .

Suddenly, Michael spoke. "Caitlin says that when you grow up, you're not afraid of the dark anymore. Is that true?"

"Yes," Kyle lied.

"Why not?"

Kyle hesitated. "Because you grow up and realize there's nothing to be afraid of."

Michael, unsurprisingly, saw through him. "Then why are you still afraid?"

That was a question Kyle had been asking himself for many years now. "Because old habits die hard."

As Michael stared at him, Kyle found himself suddenly at a loss for words. He shoved his hands into his pockets, for lack of anything better to do, and his hand closed around his keys.

He smiled. "You want to see something?"

Michael nodded.

Kyle pulled out his key chain, which had his numerous house keys, as well as the casino keys that, had he known Kyle still had copies, MacDougan would kill him for possessing. Also attached to the key chain was a green glow stick.

Removing the glow stick from the chain, Kyle said, "This is my peace of mind."

"Huh?"

"My peace of mind," Kyle repeated, "the thing that makes me feel safe." He finished taking it off the chain and held it out to Michael. "You want to hold on to it for a while?"

Reaching his hand out from under the covers, Michael took the glow stick.

Then he looked back up at Kyle and noticed the small flashlight that he kept hooked to his belt.

"You want the flashlight, too?" Kyle asked. That was another bit of his peace of mind, but he had plenty more flashlights in his bag, as well as a smaller one in his pocket.

Besides, the kid needed it right now more than Kyle did.

As Michael took the flashlight in his other hand, he said, "She won't come in the light."

Kyle frowned, wondering who he meant. It couldn't have been Caitlin.

"Who?"

"You know who."

"No, I don't."

Michael turned the flashlight on and shone it into Kyle's face. "Yes, you do. You've seen her, too."

The kid was *really* starting to scare Kyle—and he didn't scare all that easily.

"Why would you say something like that, Michael?"

"Because it's the truth. I can tell." He turned the flashlight off. "Sometimes I think about just turning off all the lights and letting her come and take me. Sometimes I think that would be easier than being so scared. Did you ever think that?"

Kyle found himself unable to say anything. He had no idea what the kid was talking about—

(Yes, you do!)

—and couldn't form any kind of coherent reply.

"She's gonna kill me, you know."

That Kyle could respond to. "No one's going to kill you, Michael. Nothing's going to happen to you." He was about to say he wouldn't let it, but somehow he didn't think that would carry much weight, so instead he said, "Your sister won't let it."

"My sister can't stop her."

"Step away from the patient!"

Kyle whirled around at the new voice. It was one of the nurses, flanked by a couple of goons wearing uniforms with "Security" stenciled on them.

"What's going on?" Kyle asked.

Then the two goons grabbed him.

"Hey!"

"You're not authorized to be here, sir," the nurse said in that patronizing voice that nurses always used when they talked to patients they deemed trouble-makers. "Please don't cause a scene."

Kyle had spent his entire adolescence and much of his adult life to date listening to nurses talk to him like a four-year-old—and also being held by hospital security guards.

These guards didn't even have a particularly strong grip. They were bigger than Kyle, but it was all about leverage.

"Take your hands *off* me," Kyle said through clenched teeth, then punctuated his point by throwing one guard off him and grabbing one guard's wrist and twisting it behind his back.

"Kyle?" cried a familiar voice from the door.

It was Caitlin.

"You know this man?" the nurse asked harshly.

"I asked him to come," Caitlin said, never taking her eyes off Kyle.

Kyle couldn't take his eyes off her, either. For some reason, he expected her to look just as she did twelve years ago, only, well, taller. And she did look similar—it was obviously the same person—but the chubbiness had gone out of her cheeks, she'd grown her hair long, and she—

She was beautiful.

And yet, at the same time, she looked like hell. She had the look of someone who hadn't slept nearly enough lately, a look Kyle was quite familiar with, as he saw it regularly in the mirror. Her cheeks looked sunken, and her body language was almost twitchy.

The nurse shot Caitlin a look. "Are you sure?"

"Yes. Let him go, please," she said to the guards.

Of course, it was as much Kyle letting go of the guards as the other way around at that point, but Kyle loosened his grip, and the guards did likewise.

The nurse, of course, was still pissed. "Visiting hours are over. I want him off my ward."

Kyle bit back a reply as Caitlin said, "No problem."

"And next time, sign him in."

"I will. Please, it's okay." Caitlin led Kyle out of the room, probably worried that Kyle would start something with the nurse or continue what had been started with the guards.

Kyle let her do so because he himself was worried about the same thing.

She led him to a window at the top of the staircase, then said, "Wait here," and went back to the room, no doubt to make peace with the nurse. Kyle thought that was a waste of time. Nurses were the enemy as far as he was concerned, but nobody asked him.

He stood at the window, reaching into his pocket for his smaller flashlight. The window had a remarkable view of the old lighthouse—long since fallen into disuse—with the spectacular reds, oranges, and purples of the dusk sky behind it.

To most people, it would be a gorgeous panorama worthy of a painting. To Kyle Walsh, it just meant night was coming.

Absently, he flicked the flashlight on and off and thought back on Michael Greene's words.

"She's gonna kill me, you know."

The question was, who was "she"?

"What were you doing up there?"

Kyle turned to see that Caitlin had returned. He started downstairs. "You asked me to."

"I asked for *advice,*" she said, following him, "over the *phone.*"

"I was just trying—"

"He's a little boy!" she said as they reached the bottom of the stairs. "You can't just barge in and freak him out like that!"

She held something out to him—it was his overnight bag, which he had left in Michael's room.

Absently, he took it. "I was just talking to him."

"Michael talks to *me,*" she said defensively.

Kyle turned and stared at her. For a second, she was the same ten-year-old tomboy who didn't take

89

any shit from anybody and who always stood up to the bullies, whom one never made the mistake of dismissing as "just a girl"—at least not twice. Now an adult, she was channeling that energy into playing mother cub to her younger brother.

Fine. If that was how she wanted it. He had never wanted to come home in the first place. Besides, Michael's problems were way beyond Kyle's ability to fix.

No surprise there. Kyle's own problems were beyond Kyle's ability to fix, and Michael seemed even worse off, even if he hadn't actually killed anyone.

He didn't think Caitlin wanted to hear that.

At least, that's how he justified turning around and walking away from her without a word.

Caitlin chased after him. "The nurses told me there was a strange guy in Michael's room. Look, will you just stop a minute?"

Then again, maybe she *did* want to hear it. He stopped, faced her, and said, "I don't think I know how to help Michael."

Before Caitlin could process that, a familiar voice said, "Hey, Catey!"

Kyle turned to see another face he'd last seen on a little kid. This face, though, barely looked any different: Kyle's cousin Larry.

Behind his glasses, Larry's eyes went wide at the sight he saw. "Kyle?"

Wondering what he was doing here, Kyle responded in kind: "Larry?"

The cousins stared at each other for a minute. Kyle had, of course, been expecting to go through many reunions on this trip, but he'd mostly been focused on Caitlin and Michael. If he'd been asked, he wouldn't have been able to say for sure if Larry was even still living in Darkness Falls.

Yet there he was.

Larry finally broke the awkward pause by extending his hand. Kyle moved to return the hand-shake when Larry surprised him and pulled him into a bear hug.

"You came!" Larry said, patting Kyle on the back.

Kyle tried not to break the embrace too quickly, but he didn't prolong it, either.

"That's terrific," Larry said as he moved to put an arm around Caitlin—a bit too protectively, Kyle thought. "It's so good to see you." He turned to Caitlin. "I was just on my way up." Looking back at Kyle, he asked, "So is there any reason for us to panic?"

"No."

Kyle long ago learned that it was better to lie and tell people what they wanted to hear. Most people couldn't handle the truth—or if they could, they already knew it and didn't need to ask.

Larry smiled. "I keep telling Catey we've got the best doctors in the state. Hell, Dr. Murphy just got here—he graduated top of his class. In a funny kind of way, it's perfect timing."

Caitlin cringed. To his credit, Larry saw this and toned down his cheeriness.

"Well, what do you say, let me take you both out to dinner. Celebrate the prodigal's return."

Breaking away from Larry, Caitin said, "I'm going to stay here with Michael, if that's okay."

She gave Kyle one last look, then headed to the elevator.

"Caitlin," Kyle said, not wanting to let her go but knowing it was probably the smart thing to do. "I'm sorry."

Smiling sadly, she said, "Just make sure you sign in next time." Then she turned and pushed the Up button on the elevator.

"Well, cuz," Larry said with an entirely too cheerful slap on the shoulder, "whaddaya feel like?"

What Kyle felt like more than anything else was getting the hell out of Darkness Falls. "I've been here too long already. I should head out."

Larry, however, wasn't giving up that easily. "One drink?"

That was an easy dodge. "I don't drink."

"Come on, I haven't seen you in twelve years. One drink won't kill you."

No, Kyle thought, but it sure would make things entertaining.

He also knew that Larry wasn't going to take no for an answer. Besides, he *was* back home for the first time in more than a decade, and, the circumstances notwithstanding, it *was* good to see Larry again.

Giving his cousin a mock sigh of exasperation, Kyle said, "Just don't get me in trouble."

Caitlin sat in the hospital room while a nurse—not the one who had turned the light out and sicced the guards on Kyle but a different one—brought in some food for Michael.

"Okay, little buddy, it's time for your Jell-O."

Michael made a face. "I don't like Jell-O."

The nurse leaned in and pretended to whisper conspiratorially. "Want to know a secret? Nobody likes Jell-O, but nobody ever talks about it. Strange, huh?"

Caitlin smiled, and Michael's lips quivered upward a bit, which was as close as he ever came to a smile anymore.

"We'll be okay for the rest of the night," Caitlin assured the nurse.

Smiling pleasantly, the nurse departed, leaving Caitlin alone with her brother.

She reflected on how stupid it had been to call Kyle. She hadn't been sure what to expect, but him just showing up and barging into Michael's room like that hadn't been it. And he himself didn't even think he had done any good, which, in turn, made her wonder why he had even bothered to come.

More than anything, she just wanted this to be over.

"Where's Kyle?" Michael asked between bites of Jell-O.

"I don't know." Larry probably had absconded with him to some restaurant or other or maybe to Bennigan's Bar.

"Is he coming back?"

Caitlin looked down at Michael.

Michael seemed genuinely interested in seeing Kyle again. Perhaps calling him hadn't been so stupid after all.

"Maybe," she said, and turned to look out the window.

nine

Larry Fleishman practically had to drag Kyle kicking and screaming to Bennigan's Bar.

Luckily, dusk at Bennigan's was loud enough to drown out the screaming, at least.

The place was, as usual, filling up with people coming by after work—or, in some cases, still present after being there all day because they were out of work—and the ambient noise level made it impossible to converse unless you were within a few inches of each other.

Cognizant of this, the tables were all tiny, keeping the occupants close enough to be heard over the crowd noise and whatever the jukebox might be playing.

Before Larry could lead him to his favorite table, Kyle made a beeline for one table that was unoccupied, probably because it was right under one of the spotlights aimed at the nearby dance floor.

But if that was where he wanted to sit, so be it.

Larry still didn't know how he felt about Kyle's presence. Maybe it would help Michael, maybe it wouldn't—frankly, Larry was pretty doubtful. And he also wasn't sure that Kyle's presence would have a good effect on Catey—who was, ultimately, the one Larry was really worried about. In the back of his head, Larry was pretty sure that Michael was just going through a phase and would get over it before too long.

But the worry was driving Catey batshit. Larry was genuinely scared for her.

And the presence of a ghost from their childhood wasn't likely to make things any better. This town was crazy enough with ghosts as it was . . .

Right now, Kyle was glancing around the table as if he were expecting the boogeyman to leap out at him.

"Relax, buddy," Larry said. "You'll survive one drink. Beer okay?"

Kyle shook his head. "I can't."

He opened his coat and showed Larry several prescription bottles.

Larry let out a whistle. "Jesus." He sighed. "Look, one beer won't kill you. Be right back."

Before Kyle could say anything, Larry headed over to the bar, squeezing his way past a bunch of working-class folks, huddled in groups of two or three or four, attempting to converse.

At the bar itself, a bunch of guys were obviously pretty ripped. Larry guessed that they were of the unemployed-and-been-there-all-day variety. One thickly built guy was holding court on the subject of either the dot-com implosion or the performance of the Red Sox or perhaps both. Larry couldn't bring himself to give much of a shit.

He also knew the guy in question but couldn't place him. That was the problem with being a criminal attorney in a small town. You saw so many people every day . . .

"Hey, Dave," he said when the bartender came over. "Two light drafts."

"Fleishman, who's your date?"

Larry turned to see it was the thickly built guy, who apparently knew him. Not that that was such a big deal.

"My cousin Kyle."

"Kyle." The guy's eyes narrowed. "Kyle Walsh?"

"In the flesh," Larry said, as Dave brought over the beers. Larry slapped a ten down on the bar and walked off with the two beers before Dave could bring any change. It was a generous tip, more than

Larry's usual fifteen percent, but if Dave had been putting up with these louts all day, he'd earned it.

He brought the beers back to the table. Larry noticed that Kyle had centered himself in the light, as if he were as afraid of the dark as Michael.

And perhaps he was. That was part of why he wanted to sit down with Kyle: to find out precisely what was up with him these days.

"Feeling better?" he asked as he put the beers down.

No reply. Kyle just sat staring straight ahead.

Wondering if this was such a hot idea, Larry said, "Figured you'd like this. It's a light."

Again, no reply.

Sighing, Larry sat down across from Kyle and leaned in so they could hear each other.

"You shoulda told me you were coming."

Kyle shrugged. "Didn't figure you'd still be here."

"There was a lot of shit you left behind."

Another shrug. "I guess."

Larry had had clients like this: sullen, moody, unwilling to give more than the minimum necessary responses. Sometimes the answer was to try small talk.

"So, what've you been doing with yourself?"

"I'm in the, ah, gaming industry. You?"

Since Kyle was living in Vegas, Larry assumed that

meant casinos rather than, say, video games or the like.

To answer Kyle's question, Larry took on an appropriately highfalutin tone. "Larry Fleishman, attorney-at-law."

That actually got a reaction out of Kyle. "You? You're an attorney? You stole more candy from the five-and-dime than anyone else in the history of stealing."

Larry laughed. "That's why I'm a defense attorney," he said. "I can appreciate the criminal mind-set."

For some reason, that put Kyle off. He started to squirm in his chair. "Larry, I should really get going."

"What's the hurry? It's been *twelve years.* The least you can do is have one drink. You have no idea what we've been through lately."

"Yeah, well, that cuts both ways."

"Maybe."

Larry took a sip of his beer. Kyle, he noticed, had left his untouched.

"So come on, give," Larry said. "What are you *really* here for?"

Kyle seemed to resent the question. "I came to see if I could help Michael."

Laughing a *yeah, right* laugh, Larry said, "You

don't look like you can help anyone." He stared at his cousin, and he caught sight of a charm on a necklace Kyle was wearing. Larry shook his head. "Kyle, you know, she's got a whole life now."

"Who?"

"Caitlin," Larry said, though he was sure Kyle knew damn well who he meant. "This thing with Mikey has been a big burden. She hasn't been able to work. She was supposed to get third grade this year."

That got Kyle's attention. "She's a teacher?"

Larry nodded. "Yup. And a good one. The kids respond to her better. It's like she hasn't forgotten childhood the way most of us adults do, so the kids feel like they can *talk* to her, y'know?"

"Yeah," Kyle said. "Yeah, I know."

Kyle had put a lot of weight into those words, which confirmed what Larry had believed from the beginning.

There was only one reason Kyle had come back to Darkness Falls, as far as Larry was concerned, and her name was Caitlin Greene.

Ray Winchester gulped down his whiskey, then chased it with that swill from the tap that Dave called beer. He couldn't afford the good stuff—of course, strictly speaking, he couldn't afford the whiskey, either.

But what else was he supposed to do? His life was in the crapper anyhow.

Every time life kicked him in the ass, he thought it was the worst thing that could happen, and then life would turn him around and kick him in the balls.

Bad enough he flunked out of college. That got Dad all hot and fucking bothered, that his son wasn't going to carry on the Winchester tradition of lawyers. Ray had always thought that to be a crock of shit. He never wanted to be a phony-ass lawyer—he left that to punks like Fleishman. No, he wanted to work with his hands.

So he did. Until he got fired. "Laid off," they called it. "Budget cuts," they called it.

Really, though, he was just fired.

Then Marie left him. Not even to hook up with some other guy—in fact, as far as he knew, she was still single. She just didn't want to be with him anymore.

So he spent his afternoons and evenings in Bennigan's, his nights sleeping off his afternoons and evenings, and his mornings hung over. It was a nice routine, though it was eating up most of his unemployment check.

And now, the icing on the fucking cake, Kyle Goddamn Walsh comes back to town.

One of the reasons *he* was laid off, as opposed to

someone else at the plant, was that Ray was "lim-ited" in what he could physically accomplish. That was because of a back injury he had suffered when he was a kid.

Thanks to Walsh and a fucking protractor.

Next to him, Joe Tormolen must have noticed Ray tense up, since he asked, "What's wrong?"

Ray pointed at Walsh, who was sitting with Fleishman. "That guy stabbed me in the back."

"What, like with a girl?"

Joe could be such a fucking moron. "No, he *literally* stabbed me in the back."

He gulped down the rest of his beer, got up, and headed toward their table.

The rest of Ray's life may have gone to shit, but he was going to get *something* back tonight, dammit.

"Hey, jackass!" he yelled when he was close enough to be heard.

Fleishman and Walsh looked up at him.

"What're you doin' back here, man?"

"Do I know you?"

Ray felt as if he'd been punched in the gut. After all that, the bastard didn't even recognize him?

"Think protractor, asshole."

Fleishman, at least, got it. "Oh boy."

"I thought they locked you up for killing your mother."

It got a lot quieter in the bar all of a sudden.

"I don't want any trouble," Walsh said.

"Tough."

Two beers sat on the table, one full, one half-empty. Ray grabbed the full one and splashed it on Walsh.

Walsh got up and stared at Ray for a second. Ray figured this was it—finally, after more than ten fucking years, after all the physical therapy and the bullshit from the doctors, and after Marie and the job and Dad and everything, Ray was *finally* going to get a little payback.

Then the son of a bitch turned around and walked out of the bar.

Ray couldn't believe it. He turned to Joe, who was right behind him. "You see that?"

"Fuckin' pansy," Joe said.

"Yeah, well, he don't get off that easy."

Fleishman put a hand on Ray's arm. "Ray, don't—"

"Fuck you, Fleishman." Ray yanked his arm away. "He didn't come after you with any sharp objects."

"You were *kids,* for Christ's sake!"

Ray ignored the lawyer and headed for the exit.

It took his eyes a moment to adjust to the darkness of the parking lot, which was adjacent to the forest. Bennigan's was literally on the edge of town.

Once it had been the last stop before you went into the wilderness. Now it was just a nice, out-of-the-way spot for the locals to hang out, away from the dumbass tourists.

Walsh was standing under one of the streetlights that (barely) illuminated the lot, right on the far end.

"Hey!" Ray cried out as he ran toward the punk.

As he got closer, Ray saw that Walsh was holding some kind of pill bottle in his hand. Somehow it didn't surprise Ray that Walsh was a pill popper. Probably on Prozac or lithium or whatever it was they gave to psychos who stab people.

Ray ducked his head and rammed right into Walsh just as the punk said, "Ah, shit!"

The pills fell out of his hand and all over the dirt of the lot. Dave never bothered to pave the lot, figuring that the grass and dirt of the forest worked just fine.

As a result, Ray's tackle had the two of them rolling around on the ground for several tumbles—right into the underbrush.

They collided with some kind of shrub or other, and both of them clambered unsteadily to their feet.

It hadn't taken much for them to get deep enough into the forest that it was pretty much pitch dark. Still, Ray could make out Walsh's shape.

What was weird was the funny sound that suddenly started up. It wasn't the usual outside noise—crickets or seagulls or any of the other noises you heard outside at night in Darkness Falls. This was something weird.

Ray figured it was maybe a plane or something. Or maybe he was so drunk he was hearing things. Whatever.

All that mattered was beating the shit out of Kyle Walsh.

As Ray charged toward Walsh, a bright light shone in his face. Walsh had whipped out some kind of fucking Maglite or some other damn thing, and it hit Ray's eyes like a blow.

But Ray was already committed and leaped at Walsh, who swung at Ray with the flashlight.

They struggled for a few minutes like that—Walsh trying to bean Ray with the light, Ray trying to strangle Walsh.

Finally, Ray managed to knock the light out of Walsh's hands and off into the shrubs.

Walsh, though, scrambled away. He went straight for the light.

What the fuck?

Ray had no idea what the big deal was about that light, but he wasn't about to let Walsh have it. He dove for the punk and tried to wrap his arms around the bastard's neck. Walsh tried to kick him off, all the while going for that light.

That damn noise wouldn't stop. And now it was getting louder.

Walsh kicked Ray off him and got over to the light.

Then Ray saw the look in Walsh's eyes.

His eyes looked dead.

Then he saw something else.

The noise got louder.

Ray Winchester had been many things in life. He'd been happy, he'd been bored, he'd been pissed off—mostly pissed off. He'd been in love, he'd been consumed by rage, he'd been hurt.

But he'd never really been scared of much of anything.

Until now.

Until he saw the decaying *thing* that flew straight toward him in the night and ripped his chest open.

Ray Winchester screamed until he could scream no more.

His last thought was disappointment that he hadn't got to kick Walsh's ass one last time. That would've made everything worthwhile . . .

ten

1841

William Ames sat in back of Malachy's General Store, forcing himself not to be afraid.

On the one hand, he didn't want to disappoint Emma. On the other hand, he'd been hearing stories for the last year about the crazy old Tooth Fairy. He still remembered that fire up at Lighthouse Point. And he heard the grown-ups talking about how they didn't trust that lady up there, even if the other children liked her.

William was just sorry that he never got any treats from the Tooth Fairy.

His father, of course, kept saying that she wasn't a fairy of any kind, that it was just stuff and nonsense. She was just a crazy old woman who was corrupting the youth of the town, whatever *that* meant.

Father thought she should have just remarried and had children like a proper woman. Mother usually muttered something after that and changed the subject.

All William knew was that he was never able to get any treats.

"William?"

He looked up to see Emma, her pretty red curly hair sticking out from under a kerchief. The late afternoon sun shone on her curls, making her look like an angel.

Walking up to where he was sitting, she said, "William Ames, I've been looking all *over* for you!"

"I—I'm sorry, Emma. I've been waiting, like you said."

"I said to meet me in *front* of Malachy's, not behind it."

William looked down at his feet. He thought she had said the back, but he couldn't bring himself to say that, as it would make him feel even stupider.

"Is everything all right?"

"Uh-huh," William said quickly.

"Well, since no one's watching, can I see it?"

She smiled as she said it. Emma had the prettiest smile in all the town.

"If you're sure it's okay," William said, taking the item in question out of his pocket. "I kept it safe, just like you said."

He held the baby tooth out, and Emma took it, holding it up to the light.

"Oh, William, this is perfect!"

William smiled a gap-toothed smile. "Thank you, Emma. I'm glad you like it."

Emma handed William his tooth back, then grabbed his hand and led him toward the coast.

"Now, we won't be very long at all. Back in time for supper, by my estimate."

"It doesn't matter," William said happily. He would gladly spend as much time with Emma as she wanted.

It was certainly better than going home to Father.

"What about your father?" Emma asked, as if she could read William's mind. "Won't he holler and raise hell if you're not home before—" She cut herself off when she saw the look on William's face. He had cast his gaze downward. The last time he was late, Father—

He cut the thought off.

It was best not to think about Father. That would just make him unhappy and scared.

The trip they were taking was making him scared enough.

"Oh, William," Emma said, "I'm sorry. I heard about what your father did the last time you—"

"It's okay," he said quickly, not wanting to dwell on it.

"No, it isn't." Emma sighed. "We'll just have to hurry, then. We'll head over to Matilda's house, collect our reward, and be back before anyone knows we're gone."

William was just glad to spend time with Emma. And away from Father.

"Tell me the story again. I like—" He hesitated. "I like the way you tell it."

Emma rewarded him with a smile again. "All right, but only if you hurry. We don't want to keep the Tooth Fairy waiting!"

And so Emma once again told William the story of Matilda Dixon and how she tragically lost her husband at sea, then how she became known to the children of Darkness Falls as the Tooth Fairy, rewarding the children who lost their baby teeth with delicious cakes, pies, and breads.

This time, though, William interrupted the story. There was one thing he never understood.

"Nobody ever *talks* about the Tooth—about Matilda. And they get all strange whenever she's brought up."

Emma shrugged as they wended their way up the path to Lighthouse Point.

"From what I hear, folks in town thought there was something off about Matilda Dixon before her husband died. After that, they say, things just got worse."

William was about to say something else, when he suddenly lost his footing and fell over. "Hey!"

His jaw hit the dirt hard enough to hurt but not so hard that it felt like he'd broken anything.

A familiar voice said, "Look out, Willie! Why don't you watch where you're going?"

That was followed by the awful laughter.

"George Delacroix!" Emma yelled, confirming William's fears. "You know it was *you* who bumped into *us*!"

William had spent much of his life being tormented by George. He was just about the last person William wanted to see right now. He always made William feel like an idiot, and the last thing he wanted to do was feel like an idiot in front of Emma.

"Come on, Emma," George said in a much nicer voice, "I'm only foolin' with you. Besides, I came to see if you might want to come with me to the fair. It's just outside of town, they got lots of stuff, too. Candy, even a freak show." George looked down at William. William, for his part, tried to sink into the ground. "*You* might like that," George said with a sneer.

Then George suddenly reached out. William flinched—

—but George was going for something on the ground next to William.

With horror, William realized that it was the tooth, which had come loose and rolled onto the ground.

"Anyway," George said, holding up William's tooth, "somebody's gotta save you two from all this Tooth Fairy talk."

William got to his feet. He was *not* going to be George's victim again, especially not in front of Emma.

"Give it back!"

He lunged for the tooth, but George dodged out of the way. William fell to the ground again. This was getting worse.

"Aw, go on! You gonna tell your papa on me again? Little mama's boy is what *you* are."

William sat fuming on the ground. He wanted to get his tooth back, but he wasn't sure it was a good idea to confront George physically. George was bigger and faster and nastier.

"Hey, I got an idea." George knelt down next to where William had fallen. "How about you let me tell you all about the Tooth Fairy? Then you'll *really* have something to mess your britches over."

William sat there while George told the story of the fire. William knew all this—it was only a year ago, and he'd been hearing all about it.

Not that anyone really knew anything, except that there was a fire.

"The fire brigade saved the house, but she never came out."

George had a huge grin on his face as he finished the story. William, who had at this point gotten up, just wanted him to be finished so he'd go away to that stupid fair and leave him alone with Emma.

But then Emma asked, "How badly was she burned?"

"Aw, you two are nuts goin' up there. You know what I heard? After the fire, the old bat lost her mind. She got all scarred and burned. I heard she started covering up her face so no one would have to see her. So much for your pretty Tooth Fairy, huh?"

William didn't care about any of this. He just wanted George to go away.

"Awwww," George said with a vicious grin, holding out the tooth. "Don't get your knickers in a bunch, Willie. I don't want your slimy tooth any-ways. Besides, the way I hear it, it's Matilda who comes looking for teeth nowadays, and I don't need that."

This William already knew. After the fire, nobody went to Lighthouse Point anymore. It was a small miracle that the fire brigade had managed to salvage the house.

And few people had seen the Tooth Fairy. When they did, it was a glimpse only.

But the children still left their teeth for her to take. She stopped baking—probably because of the fire—so she started leaving coins instead. She always left them at night. All anyone saw of her were quick flashes in the weak light of the street lanterns.

"So you're all just wasting your time. You're not gonna get anything."

Emma stuck her finger into George's face. "You leave us be, George! No one asked you along, and William's not scared of your stories."

George hadn't lost the grin. William wished he had the courage to wipe that grin off his face.

"Sure he is. But he won't show it. Not in front of *you*, anyways. Go on, Willie," he said, shooting William a look, "tell her how much you like her."

"Shut up, George!" William hoped he wasn't blushing.

"Ah, I'm leaving anyway. I'll give you and your belle some time alone."

With that, George turned and started walking away, laughing.

William was glad to see the back of him, but he had the feeling he was going to hear that laugh for the next few hours in his head, at least.

"Belle?"

Turning, William saw Emma giving him a strange look. "Is this true, William? I—I had no idea you felt this—"

"I don't feel anything!" William grabbed his tooth off the ground where George had dropped it. "And I'm not doing this to impress you," he lied. "Let's go."

John Ames angrily snapped the bread apart as he stared with annoyance at the empty chair at the table perpendicular to him.

His wife, Martha, sat across from him, staring down at her own plate. No doubt, she thought that nothing was wrong. She always did. It drove him mad.

But not nearly as mad as that damn boy did.

Not that he was atypical or anything. Children today knew nothing about discipline. All those children going up to that—that *woman's* house and taking bad food from her, and her taking their teeth. It was morbid, and it wasn't right. That sort of thing would never have been tolerated when John was a boy, and it appalled him that the children today were being allowed to get away with it. Some were even encouraging it.

John stared at the empty chair again.

"That boy is just pushing for a taste of my belt," he muttered. "I break my back to put food on this table, and he'll eat it when I say so."

"I ain't seen William since this morning, but he swore he'd be home in time for supper," Martha said timidly. "I'm worried, John."

John snorted. "Way you coddle him, I ain't surprised."

He waited for her to elaborate, but she said nothing.

Losing patience, he said, "Spit it out, woman. You're worried, you said. Why?"

"Oh, John—he lost a tooth yesterday."

"Is that right, now?" John shook his head. Damn their eyes, he was not going to let that devil woman bewitch *his* boy.

Dinner came and went with no sign of William. It was starting to get dark.

As Martha started cleaning, John grabbed his coat.

"Where are you goin'?" Martha asked, sounding worried.

"Out," was all he said. Martha was worried enough about William.

Of course, it was precisely because of William that he was going out in the first place.

The tavern was on the edge of the forest and not far from Lighthouse Point. Many of the men from the town were there, as John had hoped. Some, he was worried, were at that ridiculous fair outside of town—full of idolators, that was—but he was grateful to see that everyone he saw was a good Christian man, and he didn't notice anyone missing who should have been there.

The first thing he did was ask if anyone had seen his boy. Joseph Montgomery said he thought he'd seen him with Emma Jackson earlier by Malachy's.

"Well, Joseph," John said, clutching a flagon of ale, "you're right about the only one who *has* seen 'im, and my wife is worried something terrible. He's not one to usually run off on his own—I raised him better than *that*—but Martha did say he lost a tooth yesterday."

A knowing look passed among the men in the bar. These were, as John had thought, good Christian men. They didn't like Matilda Dixon and her ilk. They had tolerated her peculiar behavior because she was married to a good man, but with Sonny Dixon's passing, the wife had just gotten crazier. John Ames didn't fancy having crazy people around his boy, and he knew many men in the town felt the same.

"If he's done gone where I think he's gone, well, then I think it's time we got ourselves together and put some things to *rest* around here."

John smiled at the rumblings throughout the tavern. "Yeah." "Time we took care of that woman once and for all." "Never liked the way she stayed in that house after the fire. Ain't natural." "Giving the kids money for teeth is just sick." "We should take care of her."

The men started to gather up equipment they'd need. One got a rope—after all, it might be necessary to bind her to bring her out of that damn house—and Duncan Williams, the lighthouse keeper, with help from two others, retrieved torches so they could see, since it was now dark.

Within an hour, twenty men, and even a few women, were gathered in front of the tavern. The torches were lit, casting an eerie, flickering light on the assembled multitude.

One of the men said, "I believe we should make sure that we know where they've gone. If they haven't gone to Mrs. Dixon's, we shouldn't punish the poor woman. She's been through enough."

John had to bite back a reply when he saw who it was: Reverend Pitman. Out of respect for his collar, John instead said, "Our priority is to find the children, of course, Reverend. But my son did lose a tooth yesterday, and you know how the Jackson girl likes to fill his head with stories about the Dixon woman."

Jacques Delacroix then brought his boy forward. "Go on now, *mon fils*," the large Frenchman said to little George. "Tell us what you saw. Don' be afraid, you."

John remembered that George had sometimes bullied William. Typically, instead of standing up to the boy—instead of behaving like a man—William would always come blubbering to Martha. Once he even blubbered to John. John had told him to stand up for himself.

George stood in the middle of the crowd, having removed his hat. Speaking respectfully, he said, "Yes, sir. I saw them both earlier. They were on their way up to the lighthouse. And Matilda's. I—I told them not to go, but they wouldn't listen to me."

John snarled. "That tears it, then."

"Indeed," Pitman said, heaving a sigh. "This sort of thing cannot be tolerated. Her behavior has always been extreme, even before Captain Dixon's passing."

"Let's go!" John cried, not wanting to wait any longer. Who knew what horrible things that madwoman had done to William? A weak boy such as that wouldn't last very long under the satanic ministrations of such a creature.

It took only a few minutes for them to reach the lighthouse and the charred, burned-out husk that was all that was left of the house that Captain Dixon had had built years ago.

John had heard that Matilda Dixon had taken to wearing a mask this past year to hide her face. He didn't know whether or not this was true, nor did he much care, though if it were true, it showed even more that something needed to be done about her. Preferably something permanent.

When they arrived, gathered around the entrance to the blackened structure, John could hear the waves lapping against the rocks on which the lighthouse was built.

"Matilda Dixon!" he screamed, loudly enough for her to hear. "Our children ought to be able to live in safety and peace! Now, come out so we can give them some!"

John saw movement near one of the front windows. One of the curtains moved aside, and John caught a glimpse of blond hair.

A small voice came from the window: "Don't peek."

Then the curtain closed again.

Someone threw a rock at that window, and the figure dropped to the floor.

Having had more than enough of that, John led the crowd forward to the house. She had the chance to come out willingly and didn't take it. It was time to end this.

They found her clambering to her feet, grabbing for something on one of the shelves. Delacroix and Colin O'Donnel snatched at her legs, and she fell to the ground.

As she did so, a green urn fell from the shelf and shattered on the floor.

Hundreds of teeth cascaded out. All of them were fairly small, some brown and pitted, others still pristine and white.

It was one of the most revolting sights John Ames had ever seen.

A whimpering sound came from the woman who was now facedown on the floor. "Don't peek," she muttered.

Pitman stared in horror. "Sweet Mary, Mother o' God."

John snorted. "God ain't got nothing to do with this, Reverend. Bring her out!"

Delacroix and O'Donnel turned her over.

Sure enough, she was wearing a mask. It was a porcelain one that covered her entire face, except for her blue eyes.

The madwoman put up no fight, simply muttering, seemingly to herself.

"Look at this!" Hiram Jackson came running out

of the house, holding something up. It looked like some kind of scarf. "This is Emma's! My little girl's!" Hiram had a look of pure fury on his face. "What've you done to my girl, you witch?"

All Matilda Dixon could say in her defense was, "Don't—don't peek."

Delacroix grabbed one of the ropes and tied it into a hangman's noose, then threw it over a low-hanging branch.

Originally, John had had no intention of committing violence to Matilda Dixon, but he realized that was foolish. Corrupting children was one thing, but to do what she had done . . .

John almost shuddered.

Delacroix and O'Donnel got the noose around the madwoman's neck. She was still muttering, "Don't peek, don't peek . . ."

O'Donnel yanked the other end of the rope, pulling the noose taut around the woman's neck, which, if nothing else, stopped her from saying "Don't peek" over and over again.

Even as they did this, Duncan Williams ran over to the lighthouse. John wasn't sure why.

The reverend walked up to her. "Matilda Dixon, you have been condemned for crimes committed against the children of this town." Pitman then reached out and removed the porcelain mask.

A gasp came from the preacher's throat, followed by a like noise from many in the crowd.

John was not among them. Even as Pitman got down on his knees and retched at the sight of what was left of Matilda Dixon's face, John Ames stared straight onward.

"God damn it, the whole *town's* gone soft."

John walked up to her. There were burns all over her face, half her lips weren't even there anymore, her nose was withered, and her forehead was a crackling mass of red flesh.

The only thing about her that was normal was her blond hair. That and her blue eyes, which stared at John Ames with a look of—

What?

He couldn't figure it out. He expected her to be defiant or scared, but she just looked odd.

Then he went over to the other side of the rope and pulled it all the way down, tying it to a root.

Matilda Dixon breathed her last only a few seconds later.

John turned to the crowd. "This witch whore ain't fit for no place but *hell!*"

"Ames! Stand you back!"

The voice was that of Williams, calling from the top of the lighthouse.

Looking up, John saw that the lighthouse keeper

had adjusted the giant mirror and the lamp in the lighthouse so that it would shine directly on the corpse of the so-called Tooth Fairy.

Understanding what the man intended to do, John smiled and stepped back. Meanwhile, Delacroix and O'Donnel guided Reverend Pitman, still dry-heaving, away.

Light shone down on Matilda Dixon, probably the first time true light had shone on her since the fire. Unlike the dark, foreboding, uneven light from the torches, this was a blinding, pure glare.

It was the light of God.

It was the light of righteousness.

And it burned in His glory.

Her dress caught fire first. Then her skin started to blacken. The rope also ignited, and soon the corpse fell to the ground.

A huge cheer went up from the crowd. John led it.

And then, for some reason, the cheers started to die, even as the corpse of Matilda Dixon was now a tiny inferno. John didn't understand why, until a small voice said, "Papa?"

John Ames whirled around at the familiar voice.

It was William.

Next to him was Emma Jackson, without the kerchief on her head.

Both of them were clutching items to their breasts: a piece of paper welcoming them to the fair and various sweets. Their hands were luminescent with the sticky glow of sugar candy and the black of ink.

"We—we thought—we thought we could—could make it back before supper." William was talking in a dull monotone. "We didn't—we didn't think—think we'd be so—so—so—"

And then William said nothing at all.

Neither did Emma.

They just stared at the burning corpse of Matilda Dixon.

A woman who had done nothing wrong.

John Ames felt a bit of himself die.

eleven

2002

Caitlin had had no idea how, well, vicious some of the old Grimm fairy tales truly were.

She had borrowed a big old hardbound edition of the stories compiled by the Brothers Grimm from the hospital library. It was one of those massive tomes full of old-timey engraved illustrations.

Having been weaned primarily on the Disney animated versions of a lot of fairy tales, Caitlin had been rather shocked to see how lurid, graphic, and unpleasant a lot of these tales were. People chopping off their own feet, death, destruction, removal of firstborn children . . .

She looked up at Michael, who was, miracle of miracles, asleep. His lights had gone out, so to speak, somewhere in the middle of "Cinderella."

Smiling at him, she said, "And then, when he got to the castle, he was only interested in the television remote."

Shaking her head, she closed the book with a satisfying thump, put it aside, and went over to wash her hands. The book was old and dusty and left a musty smell on her hands. She actually kind of liked it—it reminded her of when her mother read stories to her as a kid—but it didn't really fit with the sterile atmosphere of the hospital.

As soon as she finished washing and drying her hands, she looked up from the sink to see her pale, wan reflection in the mirror.

Under other circumstances, she might have thought about how awful she looked, but that was superseded by something rather more awful: Kyle Walsh, now standing behind Caitlin and looking as if he'd been rolling around in gravel.

"Hey, Cat," he said casually, as if he were bumping into her in the supermarket or something.

"What happened?" she asked, aghast.

"Coming-home party."

He fell more than sat in one of the guest chairs and just stared at the floor.

Caitlin glanced over at Michael to see that—miraculously—he was still asleep.

Then she looked over at Kyle to see that he was bleeding from a gash in his head.

"You're bleeding!" she said, hoping it would get some kind of reaction.

Kyle kept staring at the floor.

Sighing, Caitlin went over to one of the carts in the hospital room and wheeled it next to where Kyle was sitting. She also retrieved some gauze from one of the cabinet drawers.

After a moment, she hesitated, realizing that she'd obviously been spending *way* too much time in hospitals lately, if she was just helping herself to first-aid material as if she owned the place.

As she started to apply the gauze, Kyle finally moved, jerking forward in obvious pain.

"I can't help you if you don't sit up."

"Do you know what you're doing?"

"Mostly," she said, trying to keep a straight face.

He turned and looked up at her doubtfully. For just one second, he almost looked like the ten-year-old boy she had impulsively kissed half a dozen lifetimes ago.

" 'Mostly,' " he said, "does *not* inspire confidence."

She smiled wryly. "I'm not trying to inspire confidence, I'm trying to get a piece of gravel out of your scalp."

As she cleaned out his wound with tweezers and a sterile pad, she asked, "So how did this happen?"

Kyle said nothing in reply. She'd seen more lively statues.

"Okay, give me the last twelve years in twenty-five words or less."

Still staring at the floor, he said, "Went to a foster home. The Fishers. We moved out west to Vegas. Now I work at one of the casinos." A pause. "Have I hit twenty-five words yet?"

"Keep going," she said, grateful that he was talking, finally.

"Are you and Larry—"

He let the question hang.

She decided in a moment of perversity to dodge the issue just to torture him a bit. "Why do you ask?"

"I—I don't know, I just—ow!"

That last was in response to her finally dislodging one particular piece of gravel from his forehead.

Caitlin triumphantly held the gravel up in the tweezers before Kyle's eyes. "Got it. If that didn't work, I was gonna clock you over the head."

Rubbing the wound, Kyle said, "I think I would've preferred that."

Finally, for the first time since he had arrived, he looked right at her.

To her surprise, she found herself unable to hold the gaze, and so she looked over at Michael.

He was still asleep, despite the noise. Thank heaven for small favors . . .

She shook her head. "I don't know what I'm doing wrong."

"Don't give him any more tests," Kyle said suddenly.

Frowning, she said, "What?"

"They stuck me with every needle known to man, woman, or child, they gave me more Rorschachs than I could ever count, and it didn't do a goddamn thing."

Caitlin stared at him for several seconds. This was the first truly helpful thing he'd said since he arrived.

"I'm sorry you're hurt," she said in a quiet voice.

Kyle snorted. "So am I."

She raised a hand to his face. Kyle started to move his head away but then stopped. Cupping his cheek in her hand, she stared right into his eyes.

Even in Michael at his absolute worst, she'd never seen as much pain as she saw in Kyle Walsh's eyes.

Almost whispering now, she said, "I'm glad you came."

"So am I," he repeated.

Their eyes locked. Feelings that Caitlin had forgotten she had ever had—hell, had forgotten even existed—started coming to the surface.

Then the moment was shattered by a harsh male voice.

"Kyle Walsh?"

Caitlin looked up to see Officer Matt Henry, along with two other cops. The other two had their guns drawn.

"I'm gonna need you to come with me, Mr. Walsh."

"Why?" Kyle asked, though it sounded to Caitlin as if he knew the answer.

"For questioning involving the murder of Ray Winchester."

Caitlin blinked. "Ray? Ray's dead?"

"I'm afraid so, Ms.—"

"Greene. Caitlin Greene."

Matt nodded. "Right, you're going to need to come with us, also."

Caitlin looked over to Kyle, and her heart fell. Just a minute ago, he had finally started to open up, but now he was back in statue mode as he got up from the chair and followed the cops out of the hospital room.

Captain Thomas Henry loved interrogations.

It was the only part of city crime he truly

missed. Most of the time, being a cop in places like Hartford and Nashua was nightmarish, a combination of tedium, stupidity, and paperwork. And he doubted he'd ever be able to handle the sheer carnage involved in a *really* big city like Boston or Providence.

Generally, the small-town atmosphere of Darkness Falls was to his liking. Not very glamorous, but at least the crimes were generally simple and easy to deal with.

The only drawback was the relative lack of interrogations. And the ones he did do were usually pretty straightforward.

Still, he relished the challenge. The old comic books used to say that criminals were a cowardly and superstitious lot, but mostly they were just dumb as posts. However, they did have rights. Often, they didn't understand what they were even after you explained them four times, but they still had them. So the interrogation became a dance: work your way around Miranda, sidestep the legal land mines, and get yourself a confession just as the music stops.

This one was going to be a special challenge. On the one hand, it was patently obvious that Kyle Walsh had killed Ray Winchester. They were last seen duking it out in the parking lot of Bennigan's, there was a history—apparently Walsh had stabbed Winchester in the back with a protractor when they were both kids—and Walsh had a history of mental illness. A slam-dunk.

On the other hand, there was no physical evidence and no eyewitnesses to the actual murder. The medical examiner hadn't found *any* trace evidence on Winchester's body and wasn't optimistic about finding any, though the lab work would take a while. They weren't set up for murders around these parts, so the full test results would take weeks, but usually that was just a formality for the trial. There should have been *something* easy to pick up at the crime scene, but there wasn't.

So the only way this would truly be the slam-dunk that Henry knew it should be was to get a confession out of Kyle Walsh.

The interrogation room was drab and uninteresting, as all interrogation rooms should be, to Henry's mind. The centerpiece was a formica table that probably dated back to the Mesozoic Era. An old metal chair with a ripped vinyl cushion sat on one side of the table, with two newer, more comfortable chairs on the other side. Naturally, the perp sat in the crummy chair.

Henry laid out the crime-scene photos on the table right in front of where Walsh would be sitting.

He wanted to make sure that every angle of Winchester's grisly death would be visible.

On the side table, he had put out the rather startling variety of flashlights that Walsh carried either in his bag or on his person, ranging from a huge Maglite, similar to the ones the department had issued to Henry and his people, to a tiny but powerful penlight.

He also placed the six bottles of pills they'd confiscated from Walsh on the table. Then he decided to stick them in his pocket, in order to bring them out at the right moment. Interrogation was as much performance as anything, and it always paid to time things right.

Finally, he had Walsh's paperwork, which had made for some very entertaining reading.

Henry's son Matt—a good boy, who had followed in his father's footsteps—had brought Walsh in through the side entrance and had been careful to avoid the notice of Larry Fleishman. Though he wasn't a patch on the shysters you found in larger cities, Fleishman could still be a royal pain in the ass if he wanted to be. Henry's preferred method of dealing with defense attorneys was to avoid them at all costs.

With any luck, Fleishman wouldn't even know they had Walsh here.

When all was in readiness, Henry had Matt bring Walsh in. The perp had a gash on his head that the Greene woman had apparently given him some first aid for.

Walsh sat down in the "guest chair" and just stared straight ahead. If the crime-scene photos or the display of his flashlight collection had any effect on him, he didn't show it.

Henry wasn't sure if that was a good or a bad thing.

"You want to talk about it?"

Walsh shrugged. "I didn't do it."

Nodding, Henry said, "That's original. Okay, I'll play along. Do you know who did?"

Walsh didn't even dignify that with a reply. That was okay. It didn't really deserve one.

Henry walked over to the other table. "What's with all the flashlights? You afraid of the dark?"

"Yes."

The captain whirled around. He hadn't expected so blunt an answer, or one in the affirmative.

He thought that went a lot toward explaining both the hardware store inventory and the pharmacopeia.

Speaking of which . . .

"Klonopin," he said, taking one bottle out of his pocket and setting it down on the table in front of

Walsh but out of his reach. "Darvaset." He set that one down. "Shit, this one I can't even pronounce." He laid it down, then did the same with the other three.

He regarded the perp. "Doc says half of these are antipsychotics. Now, I don't know much about medicine, but it occurs to me that if a man is taking antipsychotics, it might be because he has the tendency to become, well, psychotic."

"Can I have them, please?"

Henry frowned. "You have to take them now?"

"Yeah."

An opening. "When's the last time you took them?"

"Yesterday."

A *big* opening. "Bottles say take once every six hours. You're telling me you haven't taken them in twenty-four?" He let that hang for a second, then added, "Speaking of which, the bartender says you had a beer. Not supposed to drink when you're taking prescription drugs, now, are you?"

Walsh looked away. Henry plopped down in the seat opposite him.

"That's right, Kyle, the uniform's not just for parties. I'm a real live cop. And you're a real live suspect in a real live murder."

"I told you, I didn't kill him."

Henry leaned back. "You know, I'd just *love* to take your word for it, but I keep seeing all this evidence pile up. You were the last one to be seen with the victim, and you were fighting with him at the time. Well, okay, to be fair, you were running away from him, but the point is, violence was involved. He threw your beer at you. In fact, you still reek of it. You and the victim have a history of violence."

"It was twelve years ago. I didn't even remember who he was!"

"He remembered you, though. Hard to forget someone who stabs you in the back."

Then Henry got up and picked up the folder with Walsh's rather extensive medical file. "And that was just the beginning. Stabbed your mother with scissors the same night you nailed Winchester in the back. Ward of the state mental hospital for *nine years*. Suffered from all kinds of fun things: major dissociative syndrome, night terrors. Should I continue?"

Walsh said nothing.

Henry shrugged and went on.

"Sociopathic tendencies. Attacking guards, attacking nurses, attacking yourself. Self-mutilation—cigarette burns, razor blades. Three suicide attempts."

"How?"

Blinking at the non sequitur, Henry could only

ask, "How what?" He doubted that Walsh had forgotten how he had attempted suicide.

"How did I kill Ray?"

The honest response was, *I haven't got a clue.* First rule of interrogation: Never give a perp an honest response.

"One of these flashlights oughtta do it."

"Then where's the blood? On the weapon, on my hands? You guys tested my hands, and I bet you did the lights, too—no blood, right? I admit, I haven't been back here in a few years, but I seem to recall that you still need *evidence.*"

In that moment, it all made sense to Henry. Walsh wasn't affected by the pictures because he knew it didn't matter. He already knew that they didn't have any physical evidence, so he knew they had nothing.

Henry had been thrown by the fact that he didn't lawyer up the minute he walked in. But then, he was still a psycho, even if he wasn't stupid. Maybe he liked playing games?

Either way, the interrogation was officially over. Henry wasn't going to get a confession out of him.

They'd just need to find the evidence. It had to be there *somewhere.*

After all, who else could possibly have killed Ray Winchester?

* * *

The last time Caitlin had been to the Darkness Falls Police Department, she had been a teenager on a field trip. She'd never had any need to come back since.

And she didn't like being here now. She didn't like the fact that Kyle was being treated like some kind of murderer, and she didn't like the way Matt Henry talked down to her.

She didn't believe Kyle was a killer twelve years ago, and she didn't believe it now, either.

Matt was taking her statement. "And then what did he say?"

"He told me about his foster parents."

"His foster parents," Matt repeated.

"The Fishers." Caitlin tried not to sound exasperated, and she wasn't entirely sure she was succeeding. She didn't know Matt very well, but he'd always seemed like a nice enough guy the few times they'd interacted.

She had never thought of him as obtuse before.

"He told you he had foster parents."

"Is there an echo in here?"

"Ms. Greene—"

"He's *not* a killer!"

Now Matt was sounding equally exasperated. "How do you know that? You haven't seen him in twelve years."

"Because I *know*. He's a good man."

"A good man who had foster parents."

Matt's obsession with Kyle's foster parents was getting tiresome. *"Yes."*

Then Matt passed a file over to her. "Tell me something, Ms. Greene. How do you have foster parents when you're a ward of the state mental hospital for nine years?"

Caitlin started to flip through the file with barely concealed disdain, which soon modulated to shock and, finally, to abject fear.

Words such as *psychosis, unstable, suicide attempts, shock therapy,* and more jumped out at her.

Kyle had lied to her.

She gave Matt a stricken look. "He never mentioned—"

"It's not the kind of thing you put on business cards," Matt said gently. "He's a dangerous guy, Ms. Greene. We're just lucky he didn't go off on you or your brother."

Caitlin felt the pit of fear in her stomach—already a yawning chasm after watching Michael deteriorate these last six months—grow even deeper.

She whispered, "He said he was fine."

"He lied," Matt said. "Murderers do that from time to time."

Suddenly, Caitlin found herself with a great urge to get back to Michael's side. "I—I have to get back to the hospital."

Matt nodded. "We'll be in touch."

Caitlin couldn't believe what she had read. Or that she'd been so stupid.

Why had she trusted Kyle so much, anyhow? Because she used to hang out with him when they were both prepubescent kids in a small town? Was she so desperate to help Michael that she'd—

No. It wasn't productive to go on thinking that way. She'd made a mistake by asking Kyle to come here. Ray was dead now because of that mistake. She wouldn't compound it, but she wouldn't dwell on it, either.

As she worked her way toward the squad-room exit, Kyle came out of the interrogation room with Captain Henry.

"Caitlin—" he started, reaching an arm toward her.

She stopped and glared at him. "They told me everything."

"I never meant—"

Trying to contain her fury—it didn't do to lose one's temper in the middle of a room full of cops—Caitlin said in low, measured tones, "You stay away from me. You stay away from Michael."

Then she turned to walk away. With any luck, they'd lock Kyle up, and she'd never see him again.

"Son of a bitch, you killed my Ray!"

Caitlin turned back to see that Marie Winchester had jumped Kyle from behind and was now clinging to his back while Kyle whirled around trying to shake her.

The move surprised Caitlin, considering that Marie was the one who had left Ray years ago.

But then, there was a big difference between not staying married to someone and seeing him dead.

Just as there was a difference between what you thought a person was like and what he really was.

As Matt and another cop pried Marie off of Kyle, Caitlin strode out of the squad room.

twelve

At almost four in the morning, it took Caitlin less than five minutes to drive from the Darkness Falls Police Department to the hospital.

She pulled her car into a spot right near the entrance—it was much easier to find a spot this late at night—turned the engine off, and then just sat there for a moment, holding the steering wheel.

One sniffle was all it took for the dam to break.

The cry she'd been holding in since—oh, hell, she thought, might as well admit it, holding in since Michael was first diagnosed with the night terrors—finally broke loose.

She wasn't sure how long she sat there in the driver's seat of the car, racked by uncontrollable sobs, not even bothering to wipe the tears away as they streaked down her face.

After a little while, though, she felt—not good, certainly, but better than she had before she cried. In retrospect, she wished she'd cried sooner. It might have made her think more clearly.

For example, she might have realized how stupid calling Kyle Walsh would have been.

Taking some tissues out of her purse, she pulled down the sun visor, and looked at her tear-streaked face in the mirror. She dabbed at her face. "It's okay," she told her reflection. "You can handle this. You can handle anything."

She looked up through the windshield of the car at the hospital building. All the lights were out, with one notable exception: the third-floor window of Michael's room, where the lights were, of course, still shining brightly.

Looking up at that light, she was suddenly determined to make sure that nothing bad would happen to her brother. It was a promise made in the wake of a cathartic cry, aided by the lack of sleep and the lateness of the hour, but her resolve was no less for that.

A *thunk* startled her so much she almost jumped out of the driver's seat. She did let out a quick scream.

Her head snapped to the front of the car, where a black cat had leaped onto the hood.

The cat licked its lips and stared right at her with deep green eyes.

Caitlin fell back into her seat and actually laughed. "A black cat. Thanks, God, that makes me feel *much* better."

She got out of the car. The cat kept staring at her, no doubt wondering who this strange human was and whether or not she was going to feed it.

The cat had a collar with a tag. Caitlin gingerly scooped the cat off the hood and checked the tag.

"Alfred," she read. "Okay, Alfred, let's go see if we can find your mommy and daddy."

Alfred meowed his approval.

Caitlin walked toward the hospital entrance. As she approached the ambulance bay, she heard a noise behind her.

Turning to look, she saw nothing but a mostly empty parking lot.

Thinking she was now hearing things on top of everything else, she turned back into the ambulance bay.

She heard the noise again. This time, Alfred hissed, confirming for Caitlin that she *wasn't* hearing things.

"Hey, Alfred, please tell me that's not an 'animals sense bad things before they happen' hiss."

Not wanting to take a chance, Caitlin backed

her way through the ambulance bay to the entrance, refusing to let herself be caught off-guard by anything.

So, naturally, the door opened before she had a chance to push it open with her back, and someone bumped into her, giving her her second scare in the last few minutes.

It turned out to be one of the nurses—the nice one, the one who gave Michael the Jell-O—who was obviously heading home after a long night shift.

"I'm sorry," the nurse said.

"It's okay, I'm—I'm a little on edge tonight."

The nurse looked at Alfred, then back up at Caitlin. "Are you okay, honey?"

Caitlin managed to muster up a smile for the nurse. "I can handle it. I'm just gonna see who belongs to this cat."

"We have a lost-and-found on two. They don't usually take animals, but this one looks clean, and it has a tag, so they should take it. I'm sure someone'll claim him before long. Tell them Alexandra sent you up."

Again, Caitlin smiled. "Thanks."

She watched the boy as he lay on his back.

He stayed in the light.

He'd learned that much, at least.

But he was hers now, whether he knew it or not. He couldn't stay in the light forever.

No one could.

She tried, of course. She stayed in the dark, but they brought her into the light.

The light killed her.

So she had to stay out of the light.

She never had children of her own. So she had to claim children for herself.

The boy finally fell asleep.

She became more attentive now. The mind was less resistant when asleep.

The light over the kitchen sink went out.

At that, she smiled. More darkness for her to work with.

The shadows lengthened. One of them fell over the boy's pillow.

She waited.

The boy coughed.

He rolled around on the bed.

Her heart soared. At last . . .

No, he rolled away from the shadow.

Then he coughed again and rolled toward the shadow.

At last!

At last she would be able to claim him!

As soon as he rolled into the darkness, she struck.

★ ★ ★

As soon as the elevator door to the third floor opened up, Caitlin heard screaming.

At first, this didn't concern her—people screamed in hospitals, it was simply the way it worked—and she went back to hoping that the lost-and-found people would find Alfred's owner and making a mental note to thank Alexandra the next time she saw her.

Then she made out the words: "Michael! Michael, open the door!"

It was the other nurse, the one who had sicced security on Kyle.

As soon as she registered what was happening, Caitlin ran down the hallway toward Michael's room.

The door was shut. The nurse was pounding on the door, but it wouldn't budge.

Caitlin would have thought she'd have a key, but as she approached, the nurse turned to her and said, "It won't open."

Trying the door herself, Caitlin saw that it wasn't locked, but it wasn't moving, either.

She pounded on the door. "Michael! Shout if you can hear me!"

Michael did not respond.

Caitlin tried throwing herself against the door, but that only served to add a shooting pain in her shoulder to her emotional burden.

She glanced around the hallway, and her eye fell on the fire extinguisher hanging from one wall. Grabbing it, she wielded it like a sledgehammer, smashing it against the doorknob.

"Ms. Greene, you can't—" the nurse said, but Caitlin ignored her, continuing to attack the doorknob.

It finally broke off, and again Caitlin tried to push the door open, to no avail. A barricade apparently had been built on the other side.

She did manage to crack the door open a bit, however, and saw that Michael's bed was empty.

Over the howling protests of both her shoulder and the nurse, she again slammed into the door, pushing the barricade aside and getting into the room.

About half the room was cast in shadow. About half the items in the room had been piled up against the door.

Of Michael there was no sign.

Then Caitlin saw that the door to the bathroom was closed.

"Michael!" she cried as she ran over to it, turning the handle, fearing that it, too, would be blocked.

However, it opened easily. She ran inside.

The shower curtain was drawn, but she could see

something that looked suspiciously like blood running down the inside of it.

Desperate to know what she would see and scared to death of it at the same time, she threw the curtain aside—

—to see Michael lying in a fetal position in a corner of the tub, rocking back and forth. A wicked gash was on his left arm, the blood streaking from the gash onto the tile of the tub.

He was breathing, though. In fact, he was doing so rather heavily.

The nurse finally materialized, with a couple of orderlies behind her, as well as the attending doctor.

"Out of the way, Ms. Greene, please," the nurse said. "Let us take care of him."

Caitlin backed out of the bathroom slowly, wondering when she was going to crack. First Michael, then Kyle, now this.

She couldn't take much more.

"She won't come in the light."

Since Michael Greene had first said those words to Kyle back in the hospital, they'd been echoing in his head.

He told Michael he had no idea what the boy was talking about. And he hadn't. He couldn't imagine what "she" he was referring to.

Except he did know.

He just wouldn't admit it.

The creature that hovered in the darkness. The one that whispered in your ear every time it got dark.

The one that claimed you that night.

"No," Kyle muttered to himself. Then he looked up sharply, but nobody outside the jail cell noticed.

They'd been holding him for hours—in fact, it was almost a full day now. Soon it was going to be daylight. He hadn't asked for a lawyer. He supposed he could have asked Larry to represent him, but what would have been the point? They thought he had killed Ray.

In a sense, he had.

Or, rather, *she* had.

Because as soon as they were in the dark, that was when she came out.

"Sometimes I think about just turning off all the lights and letting her come and take me. Sometimes I think that would be easier than being so scared. Did you ever think that?"

Now Kyle wished he'd told Michael the truth: that he thought it all the time. He even tried it once or twice—those suicide attempts that Captain Henry had thrown in his face.

But he'd denied that it ever happened, even to himself. It was easier that way, especially once he moved to Vegas, got as far away from Darkness Falls as he could.

The minute he got back, though, it all started again. Just as it had that night with Mom . . .

He remembered seeing the scissors. Then, as soon as he had crossed into a shadow, suddenly his mind was not his own.

Then he saw the strange, desiccated creature that looked vaguely female that had whispered, "Don't peek," even as his mother lay dying on the bathroom floor, the scissors impaling her stomach.

For years after that, she came after him, but he refused to let her in. He would not allow himself to go into the dark completely. Even as he consciously denied that she existed—and why shouldn't he? who would believe that a demon had killed his mother?—he subconsciously did everything he could to keep her away.

So she went on to another target: Michael.

Though if Ray Winchester was any indication, she wasn't done with Kyle yet, either . . .

thirteen

Caitlin was barely able to focus on what Dr. Murphy was saying to her. Her life had gone from difficult to hellish in less than twenty-four hours. Where Michael had simply been ill, now he was going crazy. There'd been a murder, and Caitlin looked to be responsible for the murderer's very presence in town.

Murphy was droning on as they walked down the hospital corridor, and she forced herself to pay attention.

"Couple of stitches, he'll be fine, but that's not my concern. Michael has no memory of the event. He did this to himself in a transient state. When a patient moves from delusion to self-mutilation, it's time to take steps."

Caitlin shuddered. The file that she'd read on Kyle also mentioned self-mutilation.

An older man approached them in the hall, and Murphy indicated him with a sweep of his hand.

"I took the liberty of contacting a specialist in Bangor. Dr. Travis?"

Travis came over and spoke in a gentle, kind voice—a welcome change from the flat, clinical tone of Murphy or, for that matter, the hardened cynical professionalism of Officer Matt Henry.

"Ms. Greene, Dr. Murphy has advised me of your brother's history and given me a chance to speak with him directly. If we could sit?"

"I'm fine standing." Caitlin had been sitting either in Michael's room or in the police squad room or in her car for most of the last few days. She preferred to stretch her legs.

"We should sit," Travis said in a firm voice that still didn't lose its gentleness.

Caitlin recognized it as an old teacher's trick: make the order sound like a nice request. Appreciating the technique, at the very least, she sat on a nearby couch, Travis and Murphy doing likewise. The cracked vinyl made an odd, almost rude-sounding noise as the three bodies settled into it.

"Your brother," Travis said, "is suffering from a highly specialized form of *pavor nocturnus,* or night terrors. Because of his consistent lack of sleep, he's suffered a psychotic break. Once the break occurs, the subject enters a trancelike state wherein he or she ceases to be able to discern what is real and what is not. Eventually, they begin to manifest a response."

"How do you mean?" Caitlin had a good idea what the answer was, but she held out a slim hope that it was just her overactive imagination at work.

"An example. A patient of mine from Pough-keepsie had a recurring dream that he could fly. One night, he got out of bed, walked to his window, and jumped out, all without waking up. He fell seven stories."

So much, Caitlin thought, for an overactive imagination.

"In Michael's case, he believes something is after him, wanting to kill him. His self-inflicted wounds are consistent with this fantasy. Now, the good news is that there is a procedure we can perform right here that has had an overwhelming success rate."

"Is it surgical?" The idea of cutting a child open filled Caitlin with disgust and was an option she would consider only as a desperate, last, life-saving resort.

"Not at all," Travis said, to her relief. "Michael will be placed in a sensory-deprivation chamber.

The boy faces his fears and realizes there's nothing to be afraid of."

Caitlin found this plan to be deeply flawed. "He hates the dark."

"That's the *point*," Murphy said, a bit acidly.

Surgery all of a sudden sounded a lot better. "What's the alternative?"

The doctors exchanged an odd look. Caitlin recognized it instantly: *The patient is not going for our preferred approach; now we have to give her all the options we don't want to do but have to tell her about.*

"Aggressive medication," Travis said after a moment, "coupled with counseling. But there's no guarantees. And in the meantime, Michael might hurt himself again more—successfully."

Caitlin squirmed on the couch, prompting another rude vinyl noise. Aggressive medication coupled with counseling was what she'd been doing for going on six months now.

"We can get the chamber from Bangor and be ready to go as early as tonight," Travis added.

Closing her eyes, Caitlin thought about Michael and the blood she had seen in the shower. She thought about the ever-increasing agony of the last six months just increasing as Michael got worse.

And she thought about Kyle Walsh and what happened to him when *he* got worse.

She did not want Michael to grow up and turn into *that*.

Opening her eyes, she said, "Do it."

Larry Fleishman's mood had started out bad when he woke up and deteriorated from there.

When he had left police HQ the previous night—after being given the usual runaround from the father-and-son tag team of Tom and Matt Henry—he had been assured that Kyle Walsh wouldn't be questioned until tomorrow, so Larry could go and get some sleep if he wanted. This was after he had assured both Matt and his father that he would be representing Kyle.

What they neglected to mention was that Kyle was already being held—they had picked him up at the hospital, then snuck him in so Larry wouldn't know he was there—and had been interrogated. Larry was sure that Kyle had been advised of his rights—the Henrys might play the usual cop mind games, but they wouldn't out-and-out break the law like that—but Larry also doubted that Kyle would bother to name him as his lawyer.

So when he showed up early the next afternoon, having spent the night tossing and turning with images of Ray Winchester's brutalized corpse dancing in his head, he was appalled to find out that he'd been duped. Worse, Kyle had been attacked by, of all people, Ray's ex-wife, Marie, who apparently had more feelings for Ray now that he was dead than she ever did when he was alive.

It took several hours to get in to see Tom Henry. Larry took that time to check in with Caitlin at the hospital. She seemed surprisingly uncaring about Kyle's fate, though she was also heavily focused on the new treatment they were going to try on Michael.

When he finally got in to see Captain Henry, along with Matt, he immediately started protesting as soon as he sat in the guest chair in Henry's office.

Henry just smiled.

"Matt told you we'd interrogate him tomorrow. That was at eleven-thirty. We started interrogating Walsh at one-thirty. Last time I checked, that made it the next day."

"Very cute, Tom."

Henry smiled. "Thank you, I thought so."

"Now I expect my client to be released immediately."

"Your client?" Henry gave his son, who stood leaning against the wall, a questioning look. "Do you recall Mr. Walsh naming Larry here as his attorney?"

Before Matt could answer, Larry said, "I'm naming myself his attorney, unless he's chosen someone else?"

The silence that followed answered Larry's question nicely.

Matt shook his head. "Dammit, he *killed* Ray!"

"You have any proof of that?"

"This is *bullshit*, Larry."

Larry leaned forward. "No, bullshit is the fact that you've kept my client locked up for sixteen hours, you interrogated him without me present, and you have yet to actually charge him with anything. On top of that, you can't produce a single piece of physical evidence linking him to the crime. Shit, he's already been attacked while in police custody. You can't even keep him safe in here!"

"It's not *his* safety I'm worried about!"

"Both of you," Henry said, "calm down."

Matt fumed.

In a much lower tone, Larry said, "Bottom line, you can't hold him for more than twenty-four hours without charging him, and you don't have the evidence to charge him. So you either turn him loose to me now, or I go to Judge Siegel and file harassment charges."

Slamming the table in frustration, Matt said, "Dammit, Larry—"

"Matt," Henry said with an undertone of warning.

Then the captain looked at Larry.

"Well?" Larry prompted.

Henry sighed, then turned to Matt.

"Kick him." Then he turned back to Larry. "Inform your *client* that we may have more questions for him. Especially once all the lab work comes back."

"When that happens," Larry said, getting up from the guest chair, "my client will be happy to talk to you—with me present."

Matt walked out of the captain's office without bothering to see if Larry followed. Larry did follow, all the way to the holding cell, where Kyle sat with that same damn blank look on his face.

After Matt opened the cage, Kyle's first question was, "Where's my stuff?"

"Lab's not through with it."

Larry sighed, wishing there was some way to avoid that, but the local lab wasn't much to work with, and for a murder, they'd have to send things to the county lab, which was quite a haul from here.

As Kyle walked toward him, Larry said, "I believe the words you're looking for are *thank you.*"

Kyle said nothing but simply pushed past Larry and walked out into the street.

It was already late afternoon, almost a full twenty-four hours since Larry had the silly idea of taking Kyle out for a drink, and the sun was starting to go down.

Although Kyle seemed to be walking with a purpose, Larry couldn't imagine what it was. He had nowhere to go, after all. His time in Darkness Falls had been spent either in the hospital, in the bar, or in a holding cell.

"You want to tell me where we're going?"

He continued to say nothing but kept moving—toward, Larry realized, a hardware store.

Larry watched as Kyle grabbed a gym bag and then proceeded to relieve the store of one of each type of flashlight it had. He also asked the clerk for a few other items that were in the back—which was, Larry noted, the first time Kyle had spoken since leaving police custody.

"Y'know," Larry said, "this isn't exactly the sort of thing that inspires confidence in your lawyer."

Still, Kyle said nothing.

But his eyes looked different.

They weren't dead anymore. They were, however, scared.

The clerk returned from the back area carrying a box of glow sticks and a high-tech lantern that looked as if it belonged in a *Star Trek* episode.

As Kyle looked over the lantern, the clerk said, "That's the shit, ain't it? Shine a spot on the damn moon. Hunters use 'em at night, mostly." He pointed at one of the many indicators on the thing.

"Even has a gauge to tell you when the battery's running down. Cool, huh?"

"Not for three hundred bucks," Larry said, noting the price tag and thinking that it was indeed "the shit," as in "piece of." Then he looked at Kyle. "These make you feel better?"

"Yeah," Kyle said as he handed the clerk his credit card. Then he took a look at his watch.

Larry wondered if he had some kind of pressing appointment or something.

" 'Cause," Larry said, "if they don't, we can run down to the old five-and-dime and pick up a shit-load of rabbit's feet and four-leaf clovers for you."

Kyle gave that the response it admittedly deserved: more silence. He signed the credit-card slip, placed the glow sticks and flashlights in the gym bag, and then hefted it.

Finally, Kyle said something to Larry. "Where're you parked?"

Larry blinked. Then he pointed at his Lexus. "Right over there."

As Kyle made a beeline for the car, Larry asked, "Okay, now what?" He also took out his keys, unlocking the door with the remote.

Kyle got in the passenger's side door and looked at his watch. Larry got in the driver's side and gave Kyle an expectant look.

"It's five thirty-six P.M. Sunset is in twenty-two minutes. You have exactly twenty-two minutes to get me to the hospital."

On the list of things Larry expected Kyle to say, that was somewhat low.

Then Kyle pulled out the gun.

Larry started. Somehow he'd missed that in the array of flashlights and batteries and gym bags that Kyle had purchased at the hardware store.

Kyle didn't make any threatening moves—he was just checking the clip to make sure it was full—but Larry suddenly realized that he should probably do whatever Kyle wanted.

Blowing out a long breath, Larry closed the door and started up the car.

As he wended his way down Main Street, he forced himself to ask the question he usually never asked his clients.

"Did you kill Ray?"

No reply.

"Kyle?"

"I don't know, okay?"

For the second time in as many minutes, Kyle replied in a way Larry hadn't been expecting.

"You don't *know?*"

"I have these things, these night terrors. I don't know what's real or what's not. It's a blank."

"I guess it's safe to say you're not over it," Larry muttered. Why Kyle couldn't have just said that on the phone when Caitlin called, Larry wasn't sure. But there was nothing to be done about it right now.

"This isn't the way to the hospital, Lar," Kyle said with an intensity that scared Larry as much as anything—and he'd been scared quite a bit these last twenty-four hours.

Larry ignored him. "You try and be a good guy," he muttered as he took a turn so fast his tires squealed. "You try and do right by your family. And what happens? You end up playing chauffeur to your possibly-serial-killing cousin. I ask you, is that fair?"

"Faster, Lar."

"Believe me, I'm trying!"

A car coming in the other direction nearly swerved off the road to avoid hitting the speeding bullet that Larry's Lexus had become.

"Why'd you have to come back, man? Everything would have worked out fine if you never came back."

"I'm sorry." To Larry's surprise, Kyle sounded as if he meant it.

Larry, however, was on a roll. "Do you know how long I've been trying to get through to her?

First it was her brother always there, and then the ghost—"

Kyle whirled and looked at Larry. "Ghost?"

"You! No one in this town had a chance with her. She never got you out of her head. All she could ever think about was *you.* You guys were only ten years old, for Chrissakes . . ."

"I just wanted to help Michael," Kyle said in as small a voice as he'd used since arriving.

"Michael's gonna be fine. They're putting him in a sensory dep tank, gonna shut out the lights, show him there's nothing to be scared of."

Again, Kyle whirled toward Larry, this time looking horrified. "They're going to put him in the *dark?"*

"They're gonna *fix* him. Tonight. Hell, maybe this'll work on you, too. You should consider it."

Larry turned a corner and almost crashed the Lexus into an orange Detour sign. He slammed his right foot on the brake, the tires squealed, and he and Kyle both jerked forward.

The car stopped well short of the sign. Larry was suddenly very grateful for his fifty-thousand-dollar car and its top-of-the-line brakes.

The sun was now most of the way below the horizon.

"Take me to the hospital, Lar," Kyle said.

To accentuate the point, Kyle raised the gun.

Larry cringed.

Suddenly, the windshield went black.

The road ahead had been nicely illuminated by the Lexus's bright headlights one minute; the next, he could see only darkness.

The headlights were still on—the dashboard lights were working just fine—but he couldn't see a thing out the windshield.

He took his foot off the accelerator, not wanting to keep going this fast, and was about to hit the brake and hoping his memory that the road had been going straight was accurate, when the windshield cleared.

The Lexus was heading straight for a very large, very intimidating tree.

Slamming his foot on the brake, Larry desperately turned the steering wheel with both hands.

Too late.

Pain slammed into Larry's ribs as the seat belt sliced into his chest and the Lexus collided with the tree. He could hear the wrenching sounds of bending metal and plastic as the grille collapsed on impact. And then he felt yet another impact on his chest, as the air bag expanded out from the steering wheel.

It was several seconds too late. Larry wondered whom he could sue to redress that particular flaw.

He crawled out of the car, his glasses having fallen off. He wiped what he thought was sweat out of his eyes, only to look down at his fingers and see that it was blood. And he heard a strange buzzing sound that he thought was a symptom of his head injury.

"All in all," he muttered, "this is turning out to be a really shitty week."

On top of this, he could have sworn that whatever it was that blocked the windshield was, well, a *woman*, oddly enough.

That couldn't have been right, though. Probably all these night terror stories from both Michael *and* Kyle, compounded with staring at Ray Winchester's mauled body, were causing his imagination to go into overdrive.

After he clambered out of what was left of his car, he reached up to grab a tree branch for support to get to his feet.

Then he realized that it wasn't a branch.

It was an arm.

The arm of the woman he'd just convinced himself was a figment of his imagination.

The buzzing grew louder.

Larry had once seen the corpse of a man who had drowned—it was one of his first criminal cases. The body barely looked human, covered as it was in the detritus of the ocean, not to mention the rather unfortunate effects of prolonged exposure to salt water on human skin.

This woman managed to look like that *and* look like a burn victim at the same time.

Unfortunately, Larry didn't have time to think about where he might have seen her before.

In fact, he barely had time to scream . . .

She had been able to claim one of them, at least.

First she broke his legs.

She was about to do worse, but then he crawled into the light that emitted from the horseless carriage.

The other one—the one who had spurned her—stood in that light, which protected him.

It protected her victim, too—or, rather, it would have, if his destroyed legs weren't still out of the light. And in the darkness. And where she could strike.

She flew down and grabbed his legs.

He screamed in pain, even as he clawed at the other one. She dragged him into the darkness.

Then she finished him.

Another dead.

Unjust? Perhaps.

But what did justice matter to her? She brought joy to the children of this wretched town, and as a reward, they hanged her and burned her.

They would pay.

She lived her life with a husband who did not give her children, and then with children who thought of her as their very own gift giver, as much a saint as Nicholas, but she came any time of the year, not just at Christmas.

And they hanged her. For nothing.

So if the man whose life she took was an innocent, what did it matter? She was an innocent, and no one came to her defense.

Many of those she'd killed over the years had been innocent. It no longer concerned her.

The other one remained in the light.

Kyle.

She had thought Kyle might be different. But he was like all the others. Fickle.

Despite the danger, she lunged at him, but the light hurt her in ways she could not begin to describe, so she pulled back.

Kyle stared up at her. Unlike most of those who saw her—those unlucky few—Kyle seemed to realize what she was.

She had always known Kyle was special.

A pity he had to die.

"Michael."

She frowned.

Kyle then got into the horseless carriage and drove off, leaving the vehicle illuminated even on the inside, keeping her at bay.

Damn him.

She followed him as he drove the vehicle—which made several wrenching noises it didn't make before—back the way it came. She could hear him talking to someone on one of those mechanical wonders that they'd come up with.

Kyle pleaded with whoever was on the other side of his conversation—apparently somebody from the healing place.

He begged them not to put Michael in the dark.

She laughed.

This would be almost too easy . . .

fourteen

In her dream, Caitlin was being pursued by a madman who had Kyle's body but Michael's face and was wielding a pair of bloody scissors.

Caitlin tripped and fell, in her dream, and then Kyle/Michael held the scissors aloft with one hand, shining a flashlight into her face with the other.

Just as he was about to plunge the scissors into Caitlin's heart, she saw that he was wearing a porcelain mask.

The scissors whizzed toward her chest—

—just as Dr. Murphy nudged her awake.

"We're almost set up," the doctor said as Caitlin sat upright on the couch. "It'll just be another fifteen minutes."

"Where's the other doctor?" she asked, rubbing the sleep out of her eyes.

"He had to get back."

"So you're going to do this?" Caitlin asked harshly, not realizing until it was too late that such a tone—and an unspoken accusation—wasn't entirely fair to Murphy.

Defensively, Murphy started, "Ms. Greene, I'm perfectly capable—"

"I know, I'm sorry," Caitlin said quickly, regretting her words.

After a moment, Murphy handed her a clipboard.

"I need you to sign these."

"What are they?" she asked, taking the offering.

"Standard consent and release of liability forms."

She shot him a look.

"He'll be fine. We have to do this for the insurance. You understand."

Caitlin nodded wearily. She'd learned more than she ever needed to know about the joys of filling out forms for the express purpose of keeping the insurance bureaucracy rolling along over the past six months.

By the time she was done skimming the forms— she wouldn't sign anything she hadn't at least given a cursory glance at—and then signing them once she was satisfied that the hospital wasn't going to claim her firstborn or anything like that, they were wheeling Michael out.

He was strapped down to a gurney—Caitlin had already objected to that precaution but had been overruled by hospital policy—and was being wheeled over to the room with the sensory-deprivation tank.

Caitlin walked beside the gurney in silence, stroking her brother's hair.

For his part, Michael stared at the ceiling. At first, Caitlin thought he had the same look on his face that Kyle had, but she forced herself to think of that as simply her overactive imagination on overdrive, especially after that dream she had.

"Don't be afraid, Michael. It'll all be over soon."

Michael just stared at the ceiling some more.

And overactive imagination be damned, the look on his face was the *same one* that Kyle had had on his face twelve years ago the night his mother died.

The night—*come on, Caitlin, you can finally admit it to yourself now*—that Kyle killed his mother.

They brought him into a room with what looked like an MRI chamber the way H. R. Giger would have designed it. Michael was set on a table that would be placed inside a wide, dark tunnel.

As the orderly prepared a hypodermic needle, Murphy said, "We need to inject him with a sedative so we can monitor brain activity."

Caitlin nodded, and Murphy took the syringe

from the orderly. Then he took Michael's arm and started to inject the IV shunt that fed directly into Michael's arm.

Suddenly, Michael's back arched off the table, and he screamed as if he were in tremendous pain.

"Hold him down!" Murphy instructed the orderly.

"What're you *doing?*" Caitlin asked, wondering what *else* could go wrong.

"There can be a burning sensation." He looked over at her. "He's not allergic to fish, is he?"

"What the hell are you *talking* about? You didn't check before—"

"Calm down, calm down—it's all in."

As quickly as he had gone crazy, Michael went limp. Murphy took the syringe out of the shunt.

Michael wasn't actually allergic to fish—or to anything else, as far as Caitlin knew—but it was still a helluva time to ask. She wished more than ever that Dr. Travis hadn't had to go back to Bangor.

She rested her hand on Michael's chest, then withdrew it in shock. Even though he was supposedly sedated, Michael's heart was going a mile a minute.

"It'll be all right," she said, the words sounding ridiculous even as she said them, but she was unable to say anything else. "It's almost over."

Yeah, right . . .

As soon as the orderly and the nurse picked Michael up to put him into the tank, he started to cry.

He put up no resistance—the sedative at work, no doubt—but he obviously did not want to go in there. And, based on his still accelerated heart rate, he was nervous as hell about it.

"Don't!"

Caitlin turned to see, of all people, Kyle. He was holding a gun on everyone in the room.

Silently, Caitlin cursed Larry. He had said he was going to get Kyle released—there wasn't any physical evidence to support a charge of murder, which may have made legal sense but sure didn't make Caitlin feel any better—but he shouldn't have let Kyle just walk in here with a gun.

"Take him out of there," Kyle said to Murphy.

For his part, the doctor looked frightened out of his wits.

"Kyle—" Caitlin started.

"Do it!"

He turned to look at Caitlin.

And then Caitlin believed that he knew what he was talking about. That whatever had haunted Kyle all these years was the exact same thing that haunted Michael now. And that they should *not* put him in the tank if Kyle said they shouldn't.

Caitlin moved to the tank and helped Michael out of it.

"Okay, the three of us are leaving," Kyle said.

This rather surprised Caitlin, and her first thought was that she would have liked to have been consulted on the matter. She had to remind herself that she and Michael were as much hostages of that gun in Kyle's hand as Murphy, the nurse, and the orderly.

"I've got a car downstairs—"

Before Kyle could continue, he was grabbed from behind by someone who expertly disarmed him and tackled him.

It was Matt Henry, who struggled to keep the squirming Kyle still on the hospital floor while another officer held a gun on both of them.

"Stop resisting!" Matt said through clenched teeth. Something in Matt's tone must have gotten through, because Kyle, just like that, stopped resisting and allowed himself to be cuffed.

As Matt hauled Kyle to his feet, he started to read Kyle his rights, but before he could advise Kyle of his right to remain silent, Kyle abrogated that right by yelling at the top of his lungs: "Don't let them put him in the dark, Caitlin! Michael's right! It lives in the dark!"

He kept screaming as Matt and the other officer took him out.

Caitlin stared at the door Kyle and the two cops had gone through for several seconds after they left, even after the echoes of Kyle's dire warnings had faded into the hospital walls.

"Ms. Greene?"

Coming out of her stupor, Caitlin looked over at Murphy.

"We can proceed now."

Noting that the doctor's voice was a good deal shakier than it had been, and also not having the first clue what he was talking about, Caitlin asked, "What?"

"With the procedure."

Caitlin stared again after the departed Kyle Walsh.

She'd been on such an emotional roller coaster these last two days. First thinking of Kyle, tracking him down, putting her hope in contacting him. Then even more confidence, thinking his arrival— and his apparent connection with Michael on first meeting—might signal something better. Then despair as his murder of Ray Winchester was revealed, not to mention the fact that he had hidden his past from her.

There was no reason for her to trust him.

There was every reason not to trust him.

Yet she said, "No."

"Ms. Greene—"

"I think Michael's had enough excitement for one day, don't you?"

Murphy apparently couldn't think of an argument for that.

Besides, it wasn't as if the tank was going anywhere. There was always tomorrow.

Right now, Caitlin needed to relax and to think. No Larry, no Kyle, no doctors, no cops, nothing. Just her and Michael for a little while.

Then, maybe, she'd be ready to try again.

Or not.

As he slammed the door of the cage in Kyle's face, Matt Henry said, "Let's see your lawyer get you out of this one."

He sounded entirely too self-satisfied as he said it. Kyle might have shared the glee if he thought it would do any good.

But Matt was happy because he thought he'd caught a murderer.

Kyle knew that the murderer was still out there.

And had been for more than a hundred and sixty years.

In response to Matt's smart-ass comment, Kyle said, "That's gonna be kinda tough, since my lawyer's in a couple of pieces out on Ponus Avenue."

"Is that a confession?"

Kyle stared at Matt for several seconds, trying to figure out how best to answer the question.

Finally, on the in-for-a-penny-in-for-a-pound logic, Kyle put his hands on the bars and stared right at Matt, hoping like hell that he sounded convincing.

"Okay, I'm gonna give this a shot. I saw something when I was ten. It looks like a cross between a drowned rat and a burn victim. Now Michael's seen it, and it's after both of us."

Matt stared right back at Kyle.

Then he took out his baton and ran it quickly across the bars. Kyle barely got his hands out of the way in time.

Sighing, Kyle said, "That's what I thought you'd say."

Matt turned to walk away. Kyle decided to keep going anyhow.

"How many unsolved murders have you had here? Not just this year but for the last hundred? How many of them involved kids, as either the perpetrators or the victims?"

Matt stopped then.

Seeing his chance, Kyle went on, talking faster.

"I saw her when I was ten. Now Michael's seen her. And she's coming for both of us!"

Matt turned around.

He hadn't hesitated because he believed Kyle. He'd hesitated because he had come to the conclusion that Kyle wasn't psychotic, he was just insane. The look in his eyes was one of pity.

"You're crazy, Walsh."

Kyle felt as if he had deflated. Of course no one would believe him. If he were Matt, he wouldn't believe it, either.

"Crazy," he said to no one in particular, "isn't what it used to be."

Matt ignored this comment, instead continuing to his desk. He picked up the phone and punched in a number.

After a moment: "Pop? We got him."

Then the power went out.

fifteen

Tonight would be the night. The prodigal had returned. The new boy was primed.

And she was tired.

It would all come together tonight.

She had taken petty revenges here and there, of course. Colin O'Donnel died in a shipwreck. Reverend Pitman left the ministry and went missing after departing Darkness Falls, never to be heard from again. Jacques Delacroix died in a mysterious accident involving shipping crates.

William Ames and Emma Jackson left a suicide note at the lighthouse. Their bodies were never found.

John Ames drank himself into an early grave. His wife committed suicide a month after her son disappeared.

The town never truly recovered. She had seen to that.

The town, however, still survived.

For a while, she was content with that, as it gave her

the opportunity to torment those who had killed her—as well as their descendants.

And any who saw her paid the ultimate price.

Few did, though. She had no idea what powers had created her, but the strength of the legend of the Tooth Fairy—a legend that only existed because of her—had shaped her new form. Just as Matilda Dixon had avoided the light in life and urged others not to peek at her hideous form, the thing that Matilda Dixon had become was forced to avoid light, and any who peeked and saw her hideous form was free for her to destroy.

For a time, it was enough. It was enough to torment and to kill and to wreak havoc on Darkness Falls.

However, it was finally time to end it once and for all.

It was a simple matter to plunge the town into lovely darkness. She had taken a long time to understand how electricity had been so completely harnessed, but after a century, she finally got the hang of it.

Michael knew.

Kyle knew.

The others, though, would never know what hit them . . .

"What in the hell is going on in my town tonight, Matty?"

Matt Henry didn't really have a good answer to his father's question as the latter bounded out of his office. Amber emergency lights bathed the squad room in an eerie low glow, enough for them to see the closets where the flashlights and lanterns were housed.

"It's just a power outage, Pop. We'll probably need to deal with looters and the like. Nothing to worry about."

Matt said those words, but he didn't entirely believe them. A glance out the window showed that *no* lights were on *anywhere* in Darkness Falls.

It wasn't natural. It *felt* wrong.

Walsh's bullshit story about a monster would have been much easier to dismiss if three different eye-witnesses hadn't sworn they saw something similar to "a cross between a drowned rat and a burn victim." They were also all sufficiently drunk that Matt was willing to discount their testimony as unreliable.

But Walsh couldn't have known about those eye-witness accounts.

Besides, there was something in the air. Something beyond the usual saltwater tinge that always hovered in every nook and cranny of the town.

"Guys?" Walsh said from the cage. "You might want to get in here with me."

As if to punctuate Walsh's point, a loud crashing sound came from the file room.

Matt glanced around. Everyone was accounted for—Drew, Batten, Hawkins, Lipinski, Pop, and Matt himself were all in the squad room—so if someone was in there, they weren't authorized.

To Andy Batten, he said, "Go see what that is."

"You go see what that is."

Great, Matt thought, *everyone's jumpy.* He had really been hoping this was his imagination, but Batten was as spooked as Matt was unwilling to admit that he was.

"Hey, I outrank you."

"Then lead by example," Batten said. "Go see what that is."

Matt decided not to bother arguing. It was probably just some kid running around loose.

At night.

When there was no history of such a thing in town in recent times.

"Take a flashlight," Walsh said from the cage.

"Shut the hell up, Walsh."

Matt sighed then. The emergency lights didn't work in the file room.

"Andy, give me your flashlight," he said reluctantly, not wanting Walsh to think Matt was buying into his crap.

Then again, maybe Johanssen had come back from his dinner break early and not told anyone and went into the file room. That room didn't have emergency lights, after all.

Matt opened the door, leaving it open, for all the good that would do. The shelves were piled high and deep here. Most of it was stuff from before 1999 when they finally got computerized. The Darkness Falls Police Department finally entered the twentieth century just in time for the twenty-first—and in time for the Y2K scare. But, while everything in the last three years was on the computer, they hadn't had the budget to put all the older stuff into the system.

Unfortunately, this meant two things. One was that leaving the door open did no good whatsoever, because there were so many shelves and bookcases full of *stuff* that ground-level light simply did not travel very far. The other was that the flashlight didn't help much beyond a few feet in front of him, either.

So far, the flashlight wasn't showing him anything he wasn't expecting: files, more files, chairs, a wall-mounted phone, some more files, boxes, yet still more files, and a window that looked out onto—at the moment—total darkness.

Matt tried not to think about how many of those files were open missing-child and child-homicide cases.

Then, out of the corner of his eye, he caught something moving toward him . . .

It leaped into the air.

Right at Matt.

Matt cried out as he quickly dropped his flash-light, unholstered his weapon, and fired a shot.

Then the figure barked at him.

Quickly reholstering his weapon, he watched as the dog ran off into the deep dark corners of the file room.

"Matt? You okay?"

Turning, Matt saw Drew, Hawkins, and Lipinski running up to him, weapons out, concerned looks on the faces that he could see as he shined his flash-light on them. Hell, he wasn't sure how many of them there actually were.

"Somebody go tell Andy I shot at his dog."

Drew looked aghast. "You shot Luca Brazzi?"

"I shot *at* him." Matt sighed. "The dog was quick. I missed him."

Matt braced himself for the inevitable.

Sure enough, all three of them burst into guffaws.

Kyle had no idea why those three goons who ran in after Matt were laughing, but he knew that it couldn't have been good. It probably meant that they found something stupid and inconsequential.

Which meant they'd let their guard down.

And then she'd get them.

Sure enough, Batten made a wiping-his-forehead-in-relief gesture and said, "I guess everything's okay."

Then Kyle saw it.

Or, rather, saw *her*.

She was heading straight for the cop.

"Batten, get in the light, now!" he cried.

Before Batten could even make a smart-ass comment, she struck.

Kyle couldn't make out the specifics—it was already pretty dark in the squad room, and she, of course, stuck to the shadows—but he did see Batten being grabbed, heard the horrible buzzing noise, then winced as he heard an awful crunching.

They were the noises he had heard when Larry died.

Matt and his three goons came running out of the file room just as the captain came back out of his office.

"What the hell happ—"

Before Captain Henry could get an answer to his question, the broken body of Officer Batten flew over his head.

Kyle caught a glimpse of her, a quick flash as she ran past the emergency lights.

"What the hell is that?"

"Kill it! Kill it!"

The cops all opened fire. The bullets tore through

everything in sight: the desks, the computers, the files, the chairs, the emergency lights, everything except her.

And then Kyle saw the pattern. She was leading the cops to fire at her near the lights.

"Don't hit the lights! It's making you shoot the lights!"

He forced himself to refer to her as an "it," even though it sounded wrong to his mind. He wouldn't give her the credit, at least not out loud.

As more lights went out—and the buzzing got louder—Kyle saw that Batten's body had landed relatively close to Kyle's cage.

And Batten had a set of keys.

Kneeling down on the floor, Kyle reached through the bars, trying desperately to get at Batten's key chain.

He tried to ignore the death screams of the cops mixed in with gunfire as she took each of them in turn.

However, at the report of what sounded like a twelve-gauge shotgun, Kyle looked up. He saw Captain Henry with the weapon in question.

"Get away from my boy."

Kyle went back to grabbing for the keys. He shoved his shoulder as far as it could go into the space between the bars. Just another inch . . .

"Pop, no!"

That was Matt. Sounded as if the good captain had got himself nabbed.

Success! His fingers closed around the key chain. He pulled it off Batten's belt and stood upright.

It took about eight days for him to unlock the door and another seven years for him to grab a couple of Maglites.

He turned them on and shone them on Matt and the creature.

For a second, Kyle could clearly see her face.

To his shock, under all the dirt and grime and maggots and decay, there was the face of a beautiful woman.

Then she ran away, shrieking, from the brightness of the Maglites, going through the door without bothering to open it first, instead tearing it right off its hinges.

Kyle and Matt stared at each other for a moment. The cop looked as if he was about to go into shock. Kyle couldn't entirely blame him—he'd just watched several of his fellow officers, including his father, get slaughtered by something that his intellect was probably insisting couldn't possibly exist.

Looking over at Matt's desk, Kyle saw his flashlights, his flak jacket, and his meds.

He grabbed the flashlights and the jacket.

He left the meds behind.

Caitlin was frustrated. Ever since the lights had gone out and the hospital's emergency lights had gone on, Michael had set up camp under the bed. He had wedged a flashlight into the boxspring, creating a pool of light under the bed, from which he would not move.

"Come on, Caitlin," he insisted. "It's safe."

"Michael, this is ridiculous." A word that applied to her entire life lately. "Come out of there!"

"No, you get under here."

She got down on all fours and reached under the bed, trying to grab him.

"Goddammit, I can't *do* this anymore!"

"Caitlin, no!"

Before Caitlin could say anything else, she heard a buzzing noise.

As she moved to go look, Michael grabbed her by the arm, pulling her further into his little pool of light.

"Don't."

Against her better judgment, she listened to him.

She heard the sound again.

"Who's there?" she asked, not really expecting an answer.

Sure enough, she didn't get one.

"This isn't funny," she said in the warning tone she'd used on her students, on the off chance that this was some kid's idea of a joke.

Then the bed squeaked.

Someone was on top of the bed.

Caitlin had a good view of the floor and had seen no feet enter the room. So how the hell—

Then the bed started, well, bouncing. It was being lifted up and slammed back onto the floor. It was as if a hunter was beating a bush to flush its quarry out.

"As long as we stay in the light, she can't get us," Michael whispered.

The banging stopped.

Silence.

Then the bed was ripped away.

Caitlin caught only a glimpse of it out of the corner of her eye but couldn't make anything out.

"Run!" Michael cried, and Caitlin didn't need to be told twice. She grabbed the flashlight, got to her feet, and, holding Michael's hand tightly, ran from the hospital room into the dim light of the corridor.

She ran all the way down until she hit a dead end.

Dammit!

There was no way in hell she was going to turn

around. She couldn't even bear to look behind her just at the moment.

Instead, she ran for the nearest door, on her right, which led to a storage room.

She locked the door from the inside.

Shining the flashlight around the room, she saw assorted hospital supplies. She also found a light switch. She tried to turn the light on, but nothing happened. The power was still out, but this room apparently didn't merit emergency lights.

Caitlin tried very hard not to think about what, precisely, had just happened in Michael's hospital room.

A shadow fell on the frosted glass of the storage room.

Then the figure knocked on the door.

Caitlin jumped, but the knock was followed by Murphy's voice.

"The backup generators are going to be out in ten minutes. We need everyone back in their rooms imm—"

"Call the police!" Caitlin screamed. "Somebody's trying to kill us!"

But Murphy's shadow simply receded, without acknowledgment.

Then she heard another noise.

Then another.

She shone her flashlight with one hand, holding Michael's hand in a tight grip with the other.

Another noise.

Caitlin backed into something that crashed to the floor and made a huge clattering sound, and she saw something out of the corner of her eye, and it looked like that thing again, and she flashed her light, but it kept getting closer, and she *ran!*

There was a second door to the storage room. She and Michael barreled through it.

Behind her, she could hear the shrieks of the— whatever it was.

She would not turn to look.

Michael did, however, and let out a blood-curdling scream.

The elevator bank was at the end of the hall. There was no way they'd make it. And yet, following some idiotic primal instinct, or maybe because she'd seen too many horror movies, she dove for the elevator, taking Michael with her, both of them sliding on the linoleum toward the doors—

—which then obligingly slid open to reveal Kyle Walsh, of all people, holding a flare.

"Hit the button!" Kyle cried.

Michael kicked up at the Door Close button.

Just as the doors closed, Caitlin heard the impact of something against the doors.

"Goddammit," Kyle muttered as the flare went out.

Michael got up and wrapped his arms around Kyle's waist. On the one hand, Caitlin wondered if it was entirely appropriate. On the other hand, she was tempted to do the same.

What the hell was Kyle doing here, anyhow?

She noticed that there was a bag full of stuff on the floor and two lamps in the shoulder straps of his flak jacket, which were both also turned on. It made Kyle look like a Mack truck standing upright on its rear wheels.

"I knew," Michael said. "I knew you'd come back."

"You came back," Caitlin added, then realized that was somewhat redundant.

"What are friends for?" Kyle asked with a tired smile.

Then something heavy landed on the elevator, shaking it and also bringing it to a halt.

Caitlin looked up, then shot a look at Kyle.

"What does it want?"

Both Kyle and Michael fixed her with a "duh" gaze.

"Oh. Right. So how do we keep it from getting what it wants?"

Before Kyle could answer, the whatever–it–was started pounding on the top of the elevator. The car started rocking back and forth, and Caitlin was quite sure that it was on the verge of plummeting to the basement.

Then the elevator light blew out in a shower of sparks. Only Kyle's shoulder lamps provided any kind of illumination.

"Get on the floor!" Kyle said.

Without hesitation, Caitlin hit the deck, as did Michael. Kyle then leaned down, covering both of them, his shoulder lamps shining on the floor, leaving the ceiling in darkness.

For a brief second, Caitlin heard and felt nothing.

Then she heard the distinctive wrenching sound of tearing metal. Caitlin was afraid to look up, because she knew what she was going to see.

Out of the corner of her eye, she saw some peculiar tendril-like things whipping at Kyle, who tried to brush them aside. Michael, for his part, was punching the Door Open button, to no avail.

Then her eye caught the duffel bag, illuminated by Kyle's shoulder lamp.

Figuring there had to be *something* useful in there, she started rummaging through it and found a road flare.

Perfect.

Caitlin still couldn't see the monster—or demon, or killer bunny, or whatever the *hell* this nightmare was—but she could see its tendrils more clearly now, flailing about like a decaying octopus.

She ignited the flare and held it up like a light saber, waving it around at the tendrils, which were kind enough to retreat into the hole in the ceiling.

Then another slamming noise.

Caitlin's stomach lurched into her throat as the elevator started to head downward much faster than it was probably designed to.

Then it crashed to the ground, and Caitlin's stomach fell down into her knees.

Amazingly, the door opened. They ran out—

—and nearly crashed into Dr. Murphy and Alexandra, the nurse who had directed Caitlin to the lost-and-found for Alfred the cat. Caitlin, insanely, found herself wondering if the poor cat's owner had been found. And, if not, what would happen to Alfred with that *thing* running around.

"What the hell is that?" Alexandra cried.

Turning, Caitlin saw the creature start to come out of the elevator door, then recoil when it was hit with the emergency lights on this floor. It screeched and retreated back up the elevator shaft.

Two seconds later, the elevator went plunging downward. Two seconds after that, she heard a hideous crunching noise that no doubt sounded the death knell of the elevator.

"The bag."

Caitlin turned to Kyle. "What?"

"The bag of flashlights. Anybody grab them?"

Having been more concerned with getting the hell out of the elevator while using the now-burned-out flare to hold the creature off, Caitlin had not done so. Neither had Michael.

"Shit." He turned to Murphy, who looked shell-shocked, understandably, all things considered. "We need to get to the lobby. How long do we have the emergency lights?"

Murphy, though, was staring at the elevator bank, his mouth hanging open, his eyes glazed.

Kyle grabbed him by the shoulders. "How long?"

Alexandra spoke. "A-another couple minutes. Maybe."

Nodding, Kyle said, "That's all we need to get out of here."

Caitlin leaned back against an office door—

—which opened, causing Caitlin to fall backward and prompting her to scream.

However, it was just the other nurse, who also screamed, not expecting someone to fall into her as she came out.

"What is wrong with you people?" Alexandra asked.

The other nurse looked straight at Kyle. "What's he doing here? I'm calling the police."

Kyle laughed bitterly. "The police are dead."

Caitlin blinked. "All of them?"

"Pretty much. Where are the stairs?"

Horrified, Caitlin was about to castigate Kyle for being so insensitive, but she stopped herself. Right now, they needed to focus on keeping themselves alive—and, she suspected, Kyle had gotten *very* skilled at compartmentalizing his feelings over the years.

No one seemed interested in answering Kyle's question. Murphy was still in shock, and the other nurse just fixed Kyle with a venomous look, probably still bitter about his first visit when he hadn't signed in.

"When this hospital goes dark, we're all dead," he pointed out.

Alexandra finally said, "Straight ahead and left, through the old wing." She hesitated. "I—I should evacuate the other patients."

"It's not after them, it's after us."

Caitlin wasn't sure why Kyle was so sure of this, but he and Michael both seemed to *know* this thing.

"As long as they stay in their rooms, they'll be fine," Kyle added.

Finally, Caitlin asked the question that had been

preying on her mind for the last ten minutes or so: "What is it?"

"I don't know," the other nurse said, even though the question wasn't directed at her. "I haven't seen it."

Kyle, however, couldn't be bothered to answer, instead following Alexandra's directions. The others did likewise, even Murphy.

They turned the corner to find a mostly dark corridor. The only light was from dim emergency lights that only illuminated a foot-wide path of light near the wall.

Shrugging, Kyle proceeded to walk carefully down that path, never straying from it, looking like a drunk driver taking a walk-the-line sobriety test.

Shaking her head, Caitlin muttered, "This just gets better and better."

"Are you out of your mind?" Murphy asked, finally getting his voice—and his attitude—back.

Then the emergency lights in the nurses' station behind them went out. Caitlin thought she saw a shadow pass near it but optimistically chalked it up to her imagination.

Never mind the fact that tonight, reality had far outstripped anything her imagination had ever been able to come up with ...

"This isn't happening," Murphy said, sounding disgusted. "I'm going back to my office."

"Fine," Caitlin said. "Get us some flashlights."

Murphy shot her an annoyed look, turned around, and stopped. He looked at the darkened nurses' station.

Then he turned back around. "Let's just hurry up."

Kyle turned around as he worked his way down along the sliver of light. "Come on."

"Go, Michael," Caitlin said, pushing her brother toward Kyle. She wanted him out of here as fast as possible. Michael started following Kyle, breaking into a run, moving as fast as his small feet would take him.

"Michael, stay as close as you can to the wall!" Kyle yelled.

Nodding, Michael ran with his head down, keeping an eye on where his feet fell and keeping his body as close to the wall as he could get it.

Alexandra went next, running quickly, not paying as close attention to where her feet fell.

Just as one of her feet strayed from the path delineated by the emergency lights, Kyle cried, "Stay against the wall!"

Something hit up against Alexandra, smashing her into the wall. Now it was her turn to scream.

But nothing happened after that. She was completely in the light, after all . . .

Caitlin ran to give her a hand. To her surprise, Murphy was right alongside her. They helped Alexandra up, a process made somewhat difficult by their need to stay within the oh-so-thin confines of the emergency lights' illumination.

Michael turned around to see what was happening, but Caitlin admonished him, "Keep going, Michael."

He turned and kept running toward Kyle.

"Take her with you," she said to Murphy once they got Alexandra to her feet.

Nodding, he guided her along, shuffling down the beam as best they could. Caitlin followed, and behind her, the other nurse brought up the rear of their bizarre, follow-the-light, single-file progression.

"Shit," she heard Kyle say. "Stop!"

"What's wrong?" Alexandra asked weakly.

"Kyle?" Caitlin asked. She couldn't see a damn thing with all these people in front of her.

"There's still about twenty feet of dark to the end of the hallway."

Caitlin closed her eyes. Her first thought was that she couldn't take much more of this. Her second thought was that she had thought that about fifteen things-she-couldn't-take-much-more-of ago. Maybe she needed to give her resiliency more credit.

"Oh, Jesus."

It took Caitlin a moment to recognize the panicked tones as belonging to the usually phlegmatic Dr. Murphy.

"In less than a minute," the doctor continued, "the only thing left'll be life support."

"Hurry!" Alexandra cried, as she looked nervously around the corridor.

Another shadow seemed to move. Then another. Caitlin really did not want to be in this corridor any longer than she had to.

Then the emergency lights started to dim some more.

"Kyle—"

"I know," Kyle said quickly, cutting off any possible admonition from Caitlin.

"Whatever you're gonna do," the other nurse said from right behind Caitlin, "do it fast!"

Caitlin couldn't really see Kyle, but she did see his arm raised, his hand holding a necklace with a sunburst on it. With a start, Caitlin realized it was the charm she'd given him twenty years ago.

Then he threw the necklace forward.

A cracking noise followed, and then the corridor seemed to be a tad—a very small tad—brighter. But any light in a storm, so to speak.

"Let's go!" Kyle cried, and she could see the top of his head running toward the end of the corridor.

Michael went next—she recognized his footfalls, coming closer together because of his shorter legs.

Then, in front of her, Murphy and Alexandra moved through what Caitlin could now see was a shaft of light provided by the lights in the stairwell beyond the door, shining through the crack made by Kyle's necklace.

Caitlin held her breath as the doctor and the nurse almost lost their balance and stumbled into the darkness. She didn't want to think about what would have happened to Alexandra if she had set more than a foot into the darkness, and the nurse and Murphy both had the same thought, obviously, as they struggled mightily to stay in the light.

"Keep moving," Kyle said.

Turning to the nurse, Caitlin said, "Go."

The nurse nodded and started down the sliver of illumination.

Then the lights went out.

"No!" Michael cried.

He started to run toward them, but Kyle called his name and grabbed his shoulder, holding him back.

The only illumination now came from the crack Kyle had made, but that was still several feet in front of her and the nurse—and right now, that may as well have been miles, because Caitlin could now feel the creature hovering right behind her, smell the fetid stench that it emitted . . .

"Don't look at her, Caitlin," Michael said.

Kyle added, "She won't kill you if you haven't seen her. Whatever you do—" He hesitated, then finished: "Don't peek."

For some reason, that reassured her. Then she remembered. It was the last thing she had said to Kyle when she left his window when they were kids twelve years ago. It was in relation to the Tooth Fairy coming for his baby tooth.

It was, to her mind, a helluva time to bring up resonances with the Tooth Fairy, but it gave Caitlin the confidence she needed to keep her eyes shut. She hadn't truly seen the creature, so maybe she'd be safe.

She could still hear the voices of the others, and she was grateful for that, as it drowned out the beating of her heart.

Alexandra said, "Hey, I saw it."

"Me, too," Murphy said.

"Is that bad?" Alexandra asked.

"Yes," Michael said with a finality that chilled Caitlin.

Another silence followed, which Caitlin couldn't stand. "How close is it?" Then she heard a buzzing sound. "Oh, God . . ."

She heard the voice of the other nurse next to

her muttering a Hail Mary. Caitlin had never been much of a practicing Catholic, but right at this minute, she thought the nurse had the right idea.

"Okay," Kyle said, "now, both of you walk toward me *very slowly,* and don't turn around."

Caitlin focused all her energy, all her thoughts, *everything* on just putting one foot in front of the other.

Desperately, she tried to think of something—anything—else, but she couldn't.

But she still hadn't attacked her, even though it was dark. Alexandra and the doctor had seen it when the elevator door opened—Caitlin had been too busy running out of it—so that explained why the nurse had been victimized when she strayed. But Caitlin had been safe.

It had to be only a few more feet.

One foot in front of the other.

She could do this.

"I didn't—"

That was the nurse.

It was followed by a blood-curdling scream that made Michael's cry when he got the syringe of sedative sound like a whimper.

The crunching sound that followed made Caitlin's heart beat so fast she feared it would burst through her rib cage.

"Keep your eyes closed, and keep coming, Cat," Kyle said. "Nothing's changed."

Caitlin had a hard time accepting that fact. The nurse—Caitlin didn't even know her name, didn't even *like* her that much—was dead. She had seen dead bodies before, of course, starting with Kyle's own mother in the body bag all those years ago.

But she'd never had anyone be killed right in front of her before.

"Just come to my voice."

She wanted to scream.

She wanted to run away.

She wanted to die.

Instead, she put one foot in front of the other, kept her eyes ruthlessly screwed shut, and moved toward Kyle's voice.

"That's it, Caitlin. Almost."

Arms reached out and grabbed her in a comforting hug. She opened her eyes to see Kyle, his face unreadable, as it was backlit by the hallway light.

"Can we get out of here now?"

"Works for me," Kyle muttered.

Kyle led the way into the stairwell. Caitlin followed, holding Michael's hand, with Murphy and Alexandra bringing up the rear.

That was where the other nurse had been before she—

Caitlin forced herself not to think about it.

Not to think about the crunching of bone and the rending of flesh that cut the horrible scream off in mid—

She forced herself not to think about it while she wasn't thinking about it.

The stairwell had three distinct pools of light. They were standing in one of them. There was one in the middle and another at the bottom of the stairs, right in front of the rear entrance to the hospital.

"You've gotta be kidding me," Caitlin muttered.

To make matters worse, the pools were getting smaller as the emergency generator continued to run down.

"Okay," Kyle said after surveying the terrain, "Caitlin goes first with Michael, then the rest of us jump it."

"*Jump* it?" Murphy asked. "Are you crazy?"

"Yup," Kyle said calmly. "Give me your coat."

Murphy stared at Kyle for a moment. Then, apparently deciding that Kyle knew what was going on more than he did—an admission Caitlin was quite sure Murphy found difficult—he shrugged out of his white lab coat and handed it to Kyle.

He put the lab coat on Caitlin and said, "Carry Michael under this, and just walk straight across the dark like you did upstairs, okay?"

She nodded. That actually made a certain amount of sense. She was immune to the monster as long as she didn't see it, and she could keep Michael safe.

At least, that sounded good in theory.

Michael climbed into her arms, and then she wrapped the lab coat around him.

"Just a walk in the park, right?" she said, trying desperately to sound confident and failing miserably.

"Yeah, Jurassic Park," Murphy muttered.

Closing her eyes, she slowly took the steps one at a time.

This time, she didn't hear anything. It was all drowned out by the sound of her own heart, which was going about a thousand beats a second.

One step. Then the next. Then the next.

But she took solace in it. After all, if her heart was beating, it meant she was still alive.

Which was more than the nurse or Ray or, if Kyle was to be believed, the city police squad could say.

Another step. Then another.

Michael shuddered in her arms. She took solace in *that* as well. You can't shudder when you're dead.

Finally, her feet found flat ground. She had reached the bottom.

Relieved, she opened her eyes to find herself standing in a pool of light right by the back entrance. She let Michael drop to the ground as she took the oversized lab coat off. Looking at Kyle, Alexandra, and Murphy at the top of the stairs, she gave them a thumbs-up.

Murphy looked at Kyle. "Is there any way she can come back and carry us over?"

Both Kyle and Alexandra gave him a look that indicated that they weren't even going to dignify that with a reply.

"I didn't think so." Murphy sighed.

"We all jump together," Kyle said. "Give it multiple targets."

Alexandra blew out a breath. "Great plan," she muttered.

"If you have a better one, now's the time."

Nobody had a better plan.

"Then let's do it."

They each backed up as far as they could to get a running start.

"On three. One, two—"

They ran to the edge of the pool of light at the top of the stairs and jumped as Kyle finished. *"Three!"*

For an instant, Caitlin lost sight of them.

She heard another blood-curdling scream just as

Murphy and Kyle landed in the middle of the staircase.

Caitlin closed her eyes and forced herself not to cry as she heard Alexandra's scream cut off by the same awful crunching sound that had ended the other nurse's screams forever.

Ray. A jackass, but still not a bad person by any means.

The nurse. Another jackass, but she was just doing her job. She didn't deserve to die just by the bad luck of being near the rest of them.

All the cops. Good men and women who had protected Darkness Falls.

And now Alexandra. She had been nice to Michael and helped Caitlin help Alfred the cat.

And who knew how many others?

Maybe Kyle's mom?

This had to stop.

Murphy was going into shock again. "Oh shit oh shit oh shit oh shit oh shit oh shit—"

"We got one more. Ready?" Kyle was maddeningly calm.

"No, I'm not *ready!*" Murphy screamed, anger replacing shock, which was probably all for the best, as anger was more conducive to his continued survival. "Didn't you see what just *happened?* If we jump again, one of us isn't going to make it!"

212

"You're right."

Murphy blinked, as if he was expecting something else. " 'You're right'? *That's* your great motivational speech?"

"We go on three." Kyle may as well have been talking about a softball game for all the emotion in his voice.

Compartmentalization again. Or maybe he really was completely crazy.

"Okay," Murphy said. "Shit. Okay. On three."

Again, they got back as far as they could for a running start.

"One, two—"

They started to run forward.

"Three!"

Again, Caitlin lost sight of them for an instant.

Again, a scream, just as a person landed in the pool of light.

It was Murphy.

Then Kyle's head and arms poked into the light as he slammed into the floor.

Instinctively, Caitlin reached for him, grabbing his arms, trying to pull the rest of his body to safety in the light.

A screeching noise came from the darkness, and then Caitlin saw it.

Saw *her*.

Because it was most definitely a "she." It may not have been human, but it looked as if it might have been once. And it was definitely female.

Then another screech, and she felt tremendous pain in her arm as the demon woman tore into her flesh and then knocked her aside, away from Kyle.

Most of Kyle's body was still in the darkness.

The creature started to pounce . . .

sixteen

Matt Henry had seen some weird shit in his time as a cop, but tonight definitely took the cake.

He'd dealt with everything from rabid dogs to bar fights to easy-to-solve homicides. He still remembered the time old Philbert Quinn took his shotgun and blew away his television when the Red Sox were eliminated in the 1999 playoffs by the Yankees—except he missed the TV and killed his wife instead. Then there was Marcus Robertson, who took to ending a night of drunken revelry at Bennigan's by stripping to his birthday suit and wandering the parking lot shouting, "I'm buck nekkid!" at the top of his lungs, a predilection that no amount of incarceration or AA sessions had been able to curtail.

And he'd dealt with all the missing persons and

child homicides that remained in the ever-growing piles of unsolved cases.

But he'd never imagined anything like that—that—that—*thing* that had killed his father and the others.

He was still having trouble wrapping his mind around the fact that he'd never see Pop again. Never listen to him grouse about the coffee or tell a perp to sit down and shut up or bring a room to attention just by walking into it.

And the guys—Steve Drew, Vance Hawkins, Kris Lipinski, Andy Batten. They'd been his comrades, his drinking and poker buddies, his *friends* for years. It boggled his mind that he wouldn't be able to share a bottle of single-malt with Lipinski or go fishing with Batten or clean Drew out at seven-card stud or watch Celtics games with Hawkins.

They'd never organize another road trip to Pawtucket to see the Red Sox farm team play.

They'd never stand over the mangled corpse of another kid without a trace of evidence leading to the killer.

Except now, of course, Matt knew who—or, rather, what—had killed those kids. And killed his father and his friends, and quite probably Ray Winchester and Larry Fleishman, too.

Even if he didn't entirely believe it.

Still, he could hardly disbelieve the evidence of his own eyes.

Walsh insisted that this thing didn't like light. It only came out in the dark, and bright light scared it off. So maybe—maybe—they could kill it with the brightest light imaginable.

In Darkness Falls, that could be only one thing.

Matt had gone to fetch what they'd need to implement their plan, while Walsh went to the hospital to get the Greene kid and his older sister. For some reason, the thing had fixated on the kid, and Walsh thought he'd need to be protected.

He parked his SUV near the rear entrance.

As he got out, he caught sight of three people. One of them was Caitlin Greene, and she was screaming.

Her arm was also bleeding.

Without bothering to think about what he was doing, Matt got back into the driver's seat, started the engine, put his brights on, and floored it to the rear entrance.

The glass shattered under the onslaught of the SUV's strong grille, and the brights shone brightly into the stairwell.

Matt caught a glimpse of something screeching and running up the stairs. He had a feeling he knew what it was.

Walsh, Caitlin, her brother, and one of the doctors—Murphy, was it?—were all sprawled on the floor.

"Get in!" Matt yelled.

The Greenes got into the backseat. Walsh and Murphy got into the set of seats behind that.

The front passenger seat was occupied by two gasoline cans—the fruits of Matt's search.

Slamming the SUV into reverse, he pulled out, turned around, and got back onto Main Street, heading toward the turnoff that would take them up the hill to Lighthouse Point.

"Did you get it?" Walsh asked from the trunk.

Matt looked into the rearview mirror to see Murphy tending to a wound on Walsh's chest.

"Yeah."

"What are you talking about?" Caitlin asked. "And I thought you were dead."

Before Matt could say anything, Walsh said, "I said 'pretty much.' Matt was the lucky one."

This, Matt thought, was a definition of *lucky* that he hadn't been aware of before. Aloud, he said, "We're headed for the lighthouse. It's got a gasoline-fueled backup system. We light that, we're in business. It's not far."

Caitlin looked out the window, shaking her head. "Power's out all over town."

"Why don't we just keep driving?" Murphy asked. "We're safe in the ca—"

The doctor was interrupted by the window behind him shattering.

Whatever shattered the window also knocked the SUV out of whack. Matt fought with the steering wheel to keep the cruiser on the road and not to veer off into someone's house or place of business.

He glanced back at the rearview mirror just in time to see Murphy yanked out of the hole where the window used to be.

Matt Henry already knew that in his dreams, he would be hearing the hideous crunching sound that the creature made when it killed someone for the rest of his life.

He didn't need to hear it again now.

But he did.

"Jesus," he muttered.

The SUV continued to buck and weave, resisting Matt's control. So much, he thought bitterly, for power steering.

Another crashing sound, and the side window next to Walsh blew in as well.

Matt's first thought was that Pop was going to kill him when he saw what shape he brought the SUV back in.

219

Then he remembered that Pop would never do anything ever again.

And the creature responsible for it was now banging around the roof of his car.

Next to him, Caitlin was leaning into the front seat, looking for something on the dash—probably the siren.

Smart girl, he thought. It was a light source on the roof, so it would probably drive her off it. Matt himself needed both hands to keep the SUV under control, so he was glad she had thought of it.

As soon as she flipped the switch labeled Siren, Matt found himself startled by a banging sound above him. He spared a glance up to see that the roof was now dented inward—right where the siren was.

"It took out the sirens," he said.

The Greene kid—what was his name, Mickey? Michael, that was it—was holding a glow stick. He probably got it from the first-aid kit in the backseat.

"We're going to need a bigger light," Caitlin said.

Walsh, Matt noticed, was feeling around in the trunk. He then came up with the flashlight he had given to Matt back in the squad room.

Hoping that would help, Matt struggled to keep the car under control. They were now headed up the road to Lighthouse Point.

He remembered sitting in Miss Pisapia's class as a kid, doing a report on Matilda Dixon, the legendary Tooth Fairy of Darkness Falls, and how she lived up by the lighthouse. Ironically, after she'd been unjustly lynched, they had burned her corpse with the lights from the now-defunct lighthouse.

It worked once, it could work again.

Unfortunately, the very defunct nature of the lighthouse—and the equally defunct nature of the old Dixon house, which had not been occupied ever since the famous lynching and finally fell to pieces years ago—meant that the road to it wasn't very well traveled. The SUV could handle the pot-hole-laden street, but it was by no means a smooth ride.

Case in point, Matt hit a sharp bump that sent everyone flying—and most everything, including the flashlight that Walsh was using to stave off the monster.

Glancing in the rearview, Matt saw the creature flying straight toward the back of the SUV.

Shiiiiiiiit!

Then Matt saw the light again. Caitlin had retrieved the light and picked it up.

They needed only a few more minutes.

Caitlin shone the light right in the creature's face. She screeched and ran off.

Then the light went out.

"Did you get it?" Michael asked.

Not answering directly, Caitlin turned to Matt as he pulled up to the entrance to the lighthouse. "You got any flashlights?"

"Just two kerosene lanterns in the trunk," Matt said, as he put the SUV into park, leaving the brights on.

From the way back, Walsh said, "That'll have to do. Everybody stay close to me, and if she shows up, run."

"Not a problem," Caitlin said with feeling.

Matt looked at Walsh, who seemed pretty goddamned calm for someone who'd watched more than half a dozen murders tonight.

"That thing killed my father, Walsh."

"Yeah, well, that thing killed my mother, so get in line. Everybody ready?"

Michael said, "Yeah."

Caitlin nodded.

Matt just shook his head.

"Let's go," Walsh said.

They each leaped out of the SUV and ran as one toward the back for the trunk where the lanterns were. Matt could hear the beeping of the SUV, indicating that he'd removed the keys without turning off the lights, but battery conservation wasn't at the top of his list of things to be concerned about just at the moment.

Unfortunately, he couldn't get his fingers to work right, all of a sudden. The key wouldn't go into the lock properly.

Matt realized that his hands were shaking.

He was a *cop*, for Christ's sake, and he couldn't even open a trunk?

"Jesus!"

Caitlin yanked the keys out of his hand and smoothly slid the key in and turned the lock, releasing the trunk.

"Sorry," Matt said sheepishly.

Walsh grabbed the lanterns and twisted the levers.

With a satisfying *woosh* of flame, the lanterns lighted, providing a steady flame within the glass housing.

Matt reached into the trunk and retrieved his father's twelve-gauge, then grabbed the gas cans out of the front seat.

Then the four of them ran for the lighthouse door.

Caitlin got there first, and she turned the knob, but nothing happened.

"Locked!"

At this, Matt actually smiled, which pleasantly

surprised him. He hadn't ever expected to smile again.

"Now, *this* I can open," he said, dropping the gas cans and pumping the twelve-gauge.

It would have been more satisfying if it was the creature who had killed his father that he was blowing to pieces with Pop's shotgun rather than an old wooden door.

Nonetheless, the visceral thrill of it proved fleetingly satisfying to Matt.

Right now, he would take all the small victories he could get.

He looked at the others.

"Always wanted to do that."

Michael—still, after all, a little kid—grinned and said, "Cool."

Walsh, though, seemed less than impressed.

"Inside."

Matt brought up the rear, letting Walsh and the Greenes go in first while he retrieved the cans.

Inside was a simple one-room apartment that had seen better decades. No one had lived here in more than thirty years, but they had left the furniture: a mothball-covered couch that was probably ugly even before it started to decay, a chair that looked even worse, a vintage 1960s TV set that probably didn't even have color, and a single lightbulb hanging from a thirty-foot cord that stretched up into the ceiling.

A spiral staircase corkscrewed up to the higher levels. Next to it was a wall panel, which Walsh made a beeline for.

Within a few minutes, the cans had been appropriately attached to the system and the right switches thrown.

"Mind telling me how you know so much about the operation of this thing?" Matt asked Walsh, who was flipping switches as if he were the lighthouse keeper himself. "I didn't think they had too many of these things in Vegas."

"Did a report on the lighthouse when I was in third grade."

"And you still remember it."

"Yup. I also remember how to hook bait, and I haven't been fishing since I was six."

Matt shook his head. "You're a man of many talents."

"One or two."

A second later, he was done.

Now they just had to go upstairs to the lantern chamber.

Slowly, cautiously, they did so, Walsh again taking the lead, Matt, the only armed one, again taking up the rear.

The huge xenon arc sat motionless in the center of the chamber, its rotating mirror encased in optic glass. In the dim, flickering light of the lanterns, it looked to Matt like a Frankenstein monster about to wake up.

Matt went to the control panel with a smile.

"If that bitch hates bright light, she's not coming in here."

He pushed the button.

Nothing happened.

He pushed it again.

Still nothing.

"Well, that's encouraging," Caitlin muttered.

"What happened?" Walsh asked.

Matt shook his head.

"Must be a leak downstairs. The gas isn't getting through to the ignition flint."

Walsh looked at Caitlin.

"You're the only one who's still safe from her."

"Not anymore. I saw her."

Matt wondered what they were talking about.

"Are you sure?" Walsh asked.

Holding up her bloody arm, Caitlin said, "Pretty sure."

Speaking with the optimism of the very young, Michael said, "It's almost sunrise. We can wait it out, can't we?"

Matt looked at the kerosene lanterns, which were already starting to die down.

Walsh did the same.

"We're not going to last that long," he said. "We have to go down there and reset it."

He was looking at Matt as he said it.

"Who's 'we'? You got a mouse in your pocket?"

"You and me."

"Hey, you're the one with the third-grade light-house paper."

"And you're the one who took an oath to serve and protect."

"Shit."

Michael now sounded nervous. "No! She'll get us!"

"There's no other way, Michael," Walsh said, kneeling down to speak to the kid at eye level. He reached into his pocket and pulled out a key chain. It had a glow stick attached to it. "But if it gets dark up here, use this. It's always kept me safe. Because I know that if it ever gets too dark, I can crack it and shake it up, and it'll light my way. You hold this over your head, and she won't come near you. We'll be right back."

Matt was impressed with Walsh's capacity for bullshit. He'd somehow managed to cast the same type of glow stick that was useless in the SUV as a lifesaver now.

More to the point, Michael bought it. He took the glow stick from Walsh's hands with the eagerness of a hungry person being handed an apple.

Then he looked up at Walsh with the heartbreaking pleading look that all little kids perfect by the time they are two.

"You promise?"

Tears were streaking down the boy's cheeks.

"I promise," Walsh said.

"You better mean it."

Matt looked over at Caitlin at those words of hers. He wasn't sure if her words were angry or affectionate.

To his shock, he realized that it was both.

Or maybe more of the latter, since they then kissed each other.

Not the reaction Matt had been expecting, especially given her attitude in the squad room earlier.

Then again, he hadn't expected Marie Winchester to be so broken up about Ray's death. Love was weird that way.

"Shouldn't taste like blood," Walsh deadpanned.

Caitlin's smile was that of someone sharing a private joke. At this point, Matt didn't really care what the joke was, he just wanted to get a move on before the lanterns died.

As they walked down the stairs, Walsh said, "If anything happens to me, don't look back. Just get up here and keep that thing off them, okay?"

"Okay." Matt let out a very long breath. "Same goes for me."

And you're the one who took an oath to serve and protect.

Matt extended a hand. Walsh shook it.

He held up the lantern.

"You want the light, or—"

"No, you carry it."

Matt bent down to pick up his father's twelve-gauge. He racked a shell into the chamber.

Then he looked at Walsh.

"This thing's gonna kill us, isn't it?"

"No, it isn't," Walsh said with the same certainty with which he seemed to say everything. "We're gonna live through this. We're gonna grow old and have kids and send Christmas cards to each other every year."

Matt almost laughed at the sheer absurdity of the image Walsh had concocted. But then, maybe the loony bin they were all going to be put in when this was over would occasionally undo the strait-jackets long enough for them to write cards to each other.

"Christmas cards. Okay."

He held the shotgun at the ready. *This one's for you, Pop.*

"Ready?" Walsh asked.

"No. You?"

"No."

That damned certainty again. Mixed with honesty. Kept things a bit spookier than Matt liked, but this whole thing was already well beyond Matt's wildest conceptions of spookiness.

As they worked their way downstairs, the moldy, decrepit smell that permeated the old lighthouse was replaced by something more insistent.

"You smell that?" Walsh asked.

Matt nodded.

"Gas all over the place."

Walsh now had a death grip on the lantern. If the flame in that thing got out, the whole lighthouse would blow.

Of course, if worse came to worse, he thought, that might be a viable option for getting rid of the big bad monster.

"She comes at you fast," Walsh said, "so be ready."

Matt did a double take. "'She'? You sound like you know her."

"She's been in my life a long time."

Matt filed that away in his mental things-I'll-deal-with-if-and-when-the-world-gets-back-to-normal compartment right next to the how-do-I-tell-Mom-what-happened? file and the Walsh-said-that-thing-killed-his-mother file.

They got to the bottom of the spiral staircase—one flight below the decaying apartment—and found the eight-foot-tall backup generator.

On top was a pipe, meant to feed the gas to the ignition. Said pipe was broken in the middle.

"See it?" Matt asked.

"Yeah." Walsh handed Matt the lantern. "Give me a boost."

Cradling the lantern with one arm—putting a flaming lantern on the gas-covered floor right now would not be wise—and setting the twelve-gauge down against the generator, Matt interlaced his fingers, providing a "strap" for Walsh to use as a stepping stone to the top of the generator.

As soon as Walsh had clambered up to the top, Matt retrieved the shotgun and held the slowly dying lantern up to provide Walsh with as much light as possible.

"I need some more light," Walsh said after a minute.

Matt looked down at the lamp, which was dying, and then moved it closer, hoping that the info Walsh remembererd from his third-grade lighthouse report was accurate.

"Just a little more . . ."

Switching the lantern to his other arm to keep it from cramping, Matt listened as he heard Walsh muck around with the pipe, trying to get it mended before all the gas they brought leaked out. It was starting to smell like the underside of a gas station.

It was deathly quiet.

And it was getting darker, as the lantern continued to die out.

Then it stopped being deathly quiet.

Matt heard a strange buzzing sound.

The last time he had heard that sound, his father was dead ten seconds later.

"Walsh?"

"Don't move."

Then Matt noticed that his left foot was out of the light.

Before he could move it, something grabbed his leg and yanked him into the darkness, forcing him to lose his grip on both the lantern and Pop's twelve-gauge.

As the talons ripped into his chest, his final thought was, *Sorry I let you down, Pop.*

seventeen

Kyle managed to keep the lantern from falling onto the floor, which was good, since if it did, it would break, and they'd all die a flaming death.

He'd spent the last two days trying *not* to get killed. It would be embarrassing for it to happen now.

Michael deserved to live.

More to the point, Michael deserved to have the life Kyle never got to have.

And Caitlin deserved to have the life that thing out there had denied Kyle's mother.

So many dead already—Ray, the cops, Matt, the two nurses, Murphy, Larry. Not to mention Kyle's mother, and all the others who had died, just so Matilda Dixon could have her revenge.

Because it *was* her. Somehow.

This town had been paying the price for lynching an innocent woman for almost a century and a half.

It was time for it to end.

The lantern light was dying.

He needed to move closer to it.

But if he did, he risked himself and/or the lantern falling over. If the former, he'd die. If the latter, they'd all die.

He'd promised Michael he'd come back.

He hated breaking promises.

Maybe he could catch the lantern before it would fall.

Maybe, if he did fall, he'd be able to keep the lantern from breaking.

Maybe pigs would fly out of his butt, and Larry, Matt, the hospital staff, the cops, and Ray would all magically come back to life and they'd all live happily ever after.

Kyle wasn't about to lay money on any of those things—in fact, just at the moment, he considered the third possibility to be the most likely.

He went for it.

The lantern fell.

So did Kyle.

His last thought before his head collided with the gasoline-covered floor was an apology to Michael for breaking his promise.

Another one saw her.

Another one died.

It was almost routine now.

Still, it was fitting that they had come back here, to the place where it all started.

Here was where she and Sonny had chosen to build their life together.

Here was where Sonny had assured her that they would start a family after "just a few more trips at sea."

Here was where Mr. Jefferson and Mr. Turley had told her that her darling Sonny was dead.

Here was where the children had come to her, offering their teeth for sweets.

Here was where the kitchen fire had destroyed her face.

Here was where Mr. Ames and Reverend Pitman and Mr. O'Donnel and Mr. Delacroix and the others had killed her for something she did not do.

And here was where it would finally end.

Kyle's lantern had fallen beside him on the floor. It had cracked but not broken. He was still in the light.

So she would go for the other boy. He would die, like the others.

As would his sister.

As would all of them.

She arrived upstairs to find that the boy and his sister were also in the light.

But the light was dying.
When it died, so would they . . .

Caitlin tried not to think about anything.

So, naturally, she thought about everything.

The screams of Alexandra and Dr. Murphy and the other nurse echoed in her mind.

The lantern grew dimmer.

As soon as it went out, they were vulnerable to the monster.

"Please, please no, come on . . ."

She chanted it like a mantra, as if somehow pleading with an inanimate object would violate all known laws of chemistry and make the lantern stay lit after the kerosene all burned away.

A snapping sound startled her, and she saw that Michael was holding the cracked glow stick over his head.

It provided an oddly comforting green light just as the lantern went out for good.

Now all that stood between the Greene siblings and a vicious death was a tiny neon green stick.

Then the world exploded.

First one window, then the other, then the third shattered. The noise was deafening.

Instinctively, Caitlin ducked down, covering her face with her arms as shards of glass flew through the room, slicing through her cardigan, her jeans, her arms, her shoes, and her skin.

She would have expected more pain. Perhaps she had gone numb.

Once the glass settled, she uncovered her face.

It was dark.

Michael was reaching down toward the floor. The glow stick had fallen into the grating.

But now it was too late.

The creature looked more like a corpse than anything. Actually, it reminded Caitlin of a zombie in a movie that she had never forgotten. It had scared her to death when she was five.

And now it was heading right toward her.

Michael screamed.

It grabbed Caitlin's leg.

All at once, her leg went numb.

She knew she was going to die. The crunching sound that had signaled the deaths of the two nurses and later of Dr. Murphy would now resound in her own ears.

Just before she died.

Then the world exploded again.

It wasn't a window this time, though, it was a lantern, and it had been thrown from the staircase and landed right below the creature.

The monster shrieked as the breaking glass freed

the fire that burned inside the lantern to spread around the floor.

Then a pair of arms scooped Caitlin up and dragged her away from the monster, who was still shrieking from the light of the flames.

It was Kyle.

Unfortunately, the triumph was short-lived. The fire from the lantern wasn't much to start with, and with the windows shattered, the wind was blowing them out.

The monster flew into the air.

The fire started flickering down.

When it died, they were dead.

Caitlin took some small solace in the fact that she had thought that before and was still breathing.

The three of them all ran for the switch.

The creature leaped toward them.

Kyle got to the switch first.

He hit it.

The lighthouse beam, a beacon meant to guide sailing ships miles away in darkness and foggy weather, came to life.

The creature screamed as it fell to the ground. It started to disintegrate.

Then it grabbed Kyle's leg. Somehow, it was still alive.

"Hit the mirror!" Kyle cried.

Frowning, Caitlin was about to ask what he was talking about, but then Michael moved.

Reaching down to grab a piece of the broken lantern, Michael heaved it and smashed it into the mirror.

That mirror had focused the light from the beacon into a beam.

Without it, the light lost direction—or, rather, gained every direction, as now it was *everywhere*. Barely a shadow remained as the intense light spread in every direction.

Caitlin had to avert her eyes . . .

Kyle blinked his eyes several times. Purple, green, and yellow spots flew before his eyes as he tried to clear his vision in the wake of the lighthouse's onslaught.

The demon was nowhere to be seen.

On the one hand, Kyle was grateful. Perhaps it was all finally over.

On the other hand, Kyle knew things couldn't be that simple. In the blinding glare of the beacon, he had not been able to make out what happened to the creature. And he'd seen enough movies in his time to know not to be sure that the monster was dead until he saw a body—and not necessarily then.

He peered around the beacon, trying to find some sign of her.

Then he heard the buzzing.

Once again, the creature swooped down and grabbed him. She started to pull him into the shadows under the beacon's terrible glare.

Somehow, she looked even worse than before. The female form that he had described to Matt Henry as looking like a cross between a drowned rat and a burn victim now looked far more like the latter than the former. Her grip was far weaker than it had been at the hospital; she moved more slowly.

She was hurt.

That gave Kyle a chance.

One of the lantern fires was burning near his arm. That arm was still covered with kerosene from the lamp that shattered when he fell from the generator shortly after Matt's untimely demise.

Kyle reached out desperately, trying to light his arm on fire—all the while trying not to think about what the (many) psychiatrists he'd seen over the last twelve years would make of his attempt of self-immolation.

Time slowed to a crawl.

The demon pulled Kyle close.

Straining against her grip, Kyle reached out to the flame.

His arm alighted.

He turned and smiled. "I see you—bitch!"

Then he shoved his arm into her chest.

The buzzing noise was overwhelmed by a deafening scream as the creature let go of Kyle—who fell to the ground with a bone-crunching thud. He quickly wriggled out of his jacket before the fire spread to parts of his anatomy less protected by textiles.

He looked up to see the demon stumble back into the light of the beacon.

Her scream grew even louder as she exploded . . .

So it ended.

This had not been the climax she had wanted for her story.

But the ending was precisely what she had come to expect.

Perhaps this would truly end it, as it had not ended before.

Before, she had died but had not been permitted to rest.

She had been able to exact revenge for the wrongs done to her in life. She had been left childless by her husband, so others would be left childless. She had been denied the right to live in peace, so she took that right from those who harassed and murdered her.

Now, though, it was over.

At last.

Now, Matilda Dixon, the Tooth Fairy of Darkness Falls, could rest.

Kyle turned off the switch.

The demon that once was Matilda Dixon had exploded into a million pieces.

With any luck, this time she'd *stay* dead.

Kyle, Caitlin, and Michael stood in the now-darkened lighthouse chamber.

It took Kyle's eyes several moments to readjust to the darkness after the place had been so flooded with light.

Caitlin stared at him with those same beautiful eyes that he had fallen in love with as a screwed-up ten-year-old.

"Is it—"

He nodded.

"It's over."

"Matt?"

He shook his head. "No."

She lowered her head.

Then she looked up again. "Is Michael okay?"

Kyle shrugged. "Other than the next twenty years he's gonna spend in therapy, yeah."

A chuckle started to escape Caitlin's mouth, but she held it in, as if she were trying to hold back a vomiting binge. Then a laugh escaped her mouth.

"I'm sorry, I—"

Then she burst out laughing.

So did Michael.

Kyle surprised himself by joining them.

He hadn't known he was still capable of laughter. It was a good feeling.

A few minutes later, they worked their way downstairs. Matt's SUV was still parked outside the lighthouse.

The sun was starting to come up, painting the sky a burst of oranges and purples.

Every day of his life, Kyle Walsh had always been the most grateful for sunrise more than any time of the day. It was when the darkness finally ended and he could feel safe.

But he'd never noticed how pretty a sunrise could be before.

He looked down at Michael.

"You're a hero now, Michael. You killed the Tooth Fairy. All the other ones are gonna be scared of you now: Santa Claus, the Easter Bunny . . ."

Michael smiled.

Then he ran for the car. "I call shotgun!"

Kyle winced, remembering Matt. An okay guy for a cop. He had deserved better.

They all did.

As Michael climbed into the passenger seat, Kyle moved toward the backseat.

"That's fine," he said. "I'm gonna take the back and pass out from blood loss."

Caitlin opened the door for him and helped him in.

Then she kissed him.

Golden raspberries.

Only better.

"So where do you want to go?" she asked.

It seemed an odd question. There would be some kind of inquiry. After all, five cops, a doctor, a lawyer, two nurses, and a drunk were all killed by a supernatural demon reincarnation of a kids' fairy tale. If nothing else, there'd be paperwork.

Kyle tried to imagine telling this story to someone.

Then he imagined what would happen next.

It wouldn't be pretty. For him, or for Caitlin and Michael. Who would believe them? All the other eyewitnesses were dead.

They had a car. True, it belonged to the Darkness Falls Police Department, but they wouldn't miss it, being dead and all. It also had two shattered windows, a dented roof, and a broken siren, but no car was perfect.

MacDougan had probably raided Kyle's Vegas

apartment of its nonexistent furnishings and valu-
able items and made a deal with the landlord to rent
it to someone else.

Still, even if one removed Las Vegas and Darkness
Falls from the equation, there were plenty of places
to go.

So where did he want to go?

He looked at Caitlin.

"Anywhere but here."

She smiled.

"Anywhere but here coming right up."

She got into the driver's seat, turned on the ignition—she had never bothered to give Matt his keys
back, which showed remarkable prescience on her
part, Kyle thought—and started driving down the hill.

Instead of turning left into town, she turned
right.

Leaving Darkness Falls, home of the famous
Tooth Fairy, behind.

Darkness Falls, five years later . . .

The boy was already half asleep.

*His father tucked him into bed, making sure to place
his freshly ejected baby tooth under the pillow.*

*"Just leave this here, young man," the father said.
"You're going to go to sleep now?"*

The boy yawned.

"Yes, Dad."

The father nodded and pulled the covers up to the boy's neck.

"And remember—don't peek."

The boy fell asleep almost instantly. The father kissed him on the top of his head and left the room.

A moment later, the mother came in.

No doubt sensing the presence of another person in the room, the boy woke up.

"Tooth Fairy?"

The mother smiled. "It's just Mommy. Go back to sleep."

Rolling over to his other side, the boy did so.

Then the mother performed the ritual: the tooth was removed and replaced with a coin under the pillow.

The mother stroked the side of her son's head gently, then departed.

As soon as the mother left, the buzzing started . . .

About the Author

Keith R.A. DeCandido is the author of numerous novels, short stories, e-books, nonfiction books, and comic books in the milieus of *Star Trek*, *Buffy the Vampire Slayer*, *Farscape*, Spider-Man, the X-Men, *Young Hercules*, *Xena*, *Magic: The Gathering*, and *Doctor Who*. Current and forthcoming work includes *Star Trek: The Brave & the Bold*, a two-book series covering all five *Star Trek* TV shows, and *Gene Roddenberry's Andromeda: Destruction of Illusions*, the first novel based on the hit series. His first original novel, *Dragon Precinct*, will be published in 2004, and he is also the editor of the original anthology *Imaginings: An Anthology of Long Short Fiction*, coming in summer 2003. Learn more than you really need to know about Keith at his Web site at DeCandido.net.